# The Overshare

**The Wrong Side of the Tracks, Volume 2**

Lexy Timms

Published by Dark Shadow Publishing, 2022.

This is a work of fiction. Similarities to real people, places, or events are entirely coincidental.

THE OVERSHARE

**First edition. July 8, 2022.**

Copyright © 2022 Lexy Timms.

Written by Lexy Timms.

# THE OVERSHARE

## By LEXY TIMMS

Copyright 2022
By Lexy Timms

THE WRONG SIDE OF THE TRACKS #2
THE
OVERSHARE
USA TODAY BESTSELLING AUTHOR
LEXY TIMMS

---

# The Wrong Side of the Tracks

The Knockback
The Overshare
The Fightback

# Find Lexy Timms:

**Lexy Timms Newsletter:**
http://www.lexytimms.com/newsletter
**Lexy Timms Facebook Page:**
https://www.facebook.com/LexyTimmsAuthor
**Lexy Timms Website:**
http://www.lexytimms.com

Want to read more...
For **FREE?**
Sign up for Lexy Timms' newsletter
And she'll send you updates on new releases, ARC copies of books
and a whole lotta fun!
Sign up for news and updates!
http://www.lexytimms.com/newsletter

# The Overshare

**OVERSHARING MIGHT RUIN your joys...**

The last thing Gavin Freeman needs is a distraction as he heads into a huge showcase tournament in Myrtle Beach. But when Star decides to skip off with some friends at the last minute, and Lila, who is staying at the same hotel competing in her own tournament, comes down sick, Gavin feels the need to take care of her.

When a biker gang from his parent's past begins to interfere in his life, it leads Gavin through a whirlwind couple of days and his bond with Lila gets so strong that it might just break him. If the gang doesn't literally break him first.

*Lila*

Lila started her trip sick and by the time she got better, Gavin had proven to be not only a great friend, but too intense an attraction to ignore. With Star being hard to talk to and dismissive of the very existence of her relationship with Gavin, Lila fights the feelings she's catching like a second dose of her cold, only way worse.

Chaos takes over on a night out and Lila feels pushed toward making a decision; should she be the better friend and walk, or follow her heart and maybe strike out?

# Chapter One

## *Gavin*

THE ONLY REASON I WOKE up was because Lila shifted in her sleep.

Rolling over to one side, she essentially freed me to move for the first time all night. I could move my arm, which had long since gone through the stage of pins and needles and settled on just being numb. I didn't mind, though. I didn't want to disturb her once she was comfortable.

But now she was curled up with her pillow, off my arm completely, but her feet tucked and pressed against my legs. I could get up and leave right then and she would probably not notice. I could walk out of the door in thirty seconds.

The problem was, I didn't *want* to go. I was comfortable, for one thing. With my arm free, I found myself sunk into the mattress and pillows in such a way that my brain was screaming for me to just shut my eyes again. To drift back to the dreamless rest.

I could stay. I could stay the rest of the night, sleeping in here and maybe going over to the couch at some point so she didn't wake up and feel awkward. Not that us both being in the bed would be inherently awkward. I was overtop of the sheets. She was under them. It wasn't like we were breaking any rules or cheating or anything.

Right?

Even aside from all that, there was a logistical problem. How the hell was I going to get back to my room without being seen? The guys were very curious about my friendship with Lila, and I had already gotten a couple of side-eyes about it from some of them. That's not to mention what the girls on her squad would say if they happened to catch me coming out of their floor, or even worse, if they caught me coming out of her room.

I could only imagine how difficult that would be for her to explain. At least without it getting back to Star in a way that would make us look guilty of something that didn't happen.

Something that most certainly couldn't happen. Because we were friends. Nothing more.

I clenched my eyes shut and tried to shake it off. I didn't have the mental capacity to go through all this right now. I had to focus on the games coming up and making sure I remembered the scouting sheets on the hitters I was going to face on the mound. There were a couple of power batters, all batting lefty, that I needed to remember specific reports on.

Oh no.

Her leg shifted in her sleep and rose up my thigh. Her knee slid up my leg and stopped just inches from my crotch. Instantly, and without any further prodding, my cock thickened and hardened. Silently, I tried to wish it away. That was the last thing I needed at this particular moment. Especially since it was already so hard that I was essentially pitching a tent in my pants and pushing the thin hotel sheet up with it.

I needed to get out of there. None of this situation was good, not if I valued my relationship with Star. Whatever relationship that was now.

If only Star had come on the trip. This could have been entirely avoided. Maybe we both would have come together to take care of Lila and then slipped away to my room. It would have been our first night together away from campus, and with the sounds of the ocean crashing through our window, we could have let our bodies explore each other.

Instead, I was lying next to her roommate, trying desperately to will a hard-on away.

A hard-on I wouldn't have had if I wasn't finding myself insanely attracted to Lila. Which was a surprise, not because she wasn't conventionally attractive or anything, but because our friendship had been pretty solid and I had been so enamored with Star. Where did all this come from? Was I really just that upset that Star hadn't come?

Lila shifted again in her sleep, and her foot left my leg. She made a moaning sound, though, and I felt my stomach clench. No, this had nothing to do with Star and everything to do with me and Lila. Something about her was making me feel like I wanted to just curl around her, hold her as she slept. And if something just happened in the middle of the night... oh well.

I had to get out. Now.

Sliding out of the bed, doing my best not to make too much noise or make the bed move too much, I got to my feet and padded over to where my shoes lay on the floor in front of the couch. I slipped them on and took one last look at Lila before snatching up my phone and key and making my way to the door.

I opened the door and peeked out. The coast was, at least temporarily, clear. The stairs were down the hall a few doors and on the right. If I could make it to the steps and into the stairwell without anyone seeing me, I was as good as gold. I could explain being in the stairwell as wanting exercise or being drunk or something.

I waited for a few seconds more. I needed to be able to slip out and shut the door quietly so Lila didn't wake up and I didn't alert anyone in any of the nearby rooms. Taking a deep breath, I slid out of the door and slowly pulled it shut. Once it clicked, I spun and sprinted on my toes toward the stairwell door. I was almost to it, my hands reaching out, when I heard the sound of a door opening behind me. It was way down the hall, but it was unmistakable, and I barreled through the door and threw myself against the wall.

As the heavy metal door slowly slid shut, voices floated over to me.

"Did you see that?"

"See what?"

"Some guy, going down the stairs in a hurry."

"Probably Chad. You know how he is. He came and knocked on my door last year in the middle of the night asking if I wanted to party. I looked through the peephole, and he wasn't even wearing pants."

"Oh my...shit, like with his dick out?"

"No, thankfully..."

The door clicked shut, and their voices disappeared. It didn't sound like they were getting any closer, so I figured they were heading to the elevator, or at least slowly enough to the stairs that I could get back to my floor easily enough.

Letting myself exhale, I took a moment and then went up the steps two at a time. The doors had thin windows in the center, and I tried to angle myself to see down the hallway before I opened it. It looked empty. I pulled the handle and stepped in.

The hallway was not, in fact, empty.

Richie, Kosuke, and the aforementioned and apparently occasionally pantless Chad were standing in the hallway, each holding a red plastic cup and turning toward me.

"Gavin?" Richie asked.

"Fellas!" I said, entirely too loudly. I made a move that I hoped looked like I was stumbling and reached out to hold on to the wall.

"Gavin, where have you been, dude? We came to your room to get you, and you weren't there," Chad said.

"I was on the beach," I said, smiling lazily and hoping it was enough to convince them.

"The beach?" Kosuke asked. "Dude, we went down there. You weren't there."

"Yeah, I was," I said, panicking a little. "I... was down there... with a... girl."

"A girl?" Chad asked, grinning. "Wait, what about Star? Cat's away, mice will play?"

My stomach turned a little. Thinking I was cheating on Star with some random girl might even be worse than if they knew the truth that I had been in Lila's room all night. At least then I could tell everyone what really happened, and if they didn't believe me, that was on them.

"S'was Star," I said, a story forming in my mind quickly. "She came to see me before she left."

"Oh," Richie said. "Right on, man. Good for you."

Kosuke reached up for a high-five, which I calculatingly missed most of.

"I thought she was already gone," Chad said, his voice a little lower so only he and I could hear him. "I know one of the other girls on that trip. I thought I saw her post a picture with all of them at the airport."

I shrugged.

"Sure looked like Star," I said and shoved the key card into the door of my room. Before Chad could form a comeback to that, I shut the door behind me and locked it.

Well, that sucked. A lot.

I walked over to the bathroom, stripping off my clothes as I did so. At least the craziness of the last few minutes had knocked off the boner. That was something in the win column.

Turning on the shower, I ran it fairly lukewarm, not wanting to give myself an easy pass for anything, and stepped inside. The cool water woke me up a bit but cleared my mind. After a few minutes, I allowed it to get warmer, and by the time I stepped out, the tension in my muscles was gone, and I was ready for sleep.

Tossing on an old pair of shorts, I crawled into the bed and stuck my phone on the charger. Setting it against the lamp, I turned on an

ASMR video that I had saved on my playlist for nights when I really needed to get to sleep and lay back.

I stared at the ceiling for a long time. I could hear guys come and go out of the room next door. Kevin was on the other side, and I was sure he was taking the night off of shenanigans. He tended to be rather responsible when it came to partying before a game, even if his barrel chest and tree-like stature meant he could drink us all under the table and barely be buzzed. The man liked his sleep. Nights before a game, he would probably be in bed by ten, and the strongest thing he would have to drink would be a glass of wine.

Letting my mind drift, I thought about how funny it was that my best friend liked a glass of wine before bed while looking like Paul Bunyan and being surrounded by guys who did liquor shots and drank beer like it was water. He stuck out, and in the best way. He was different.

A lot like Lila.

Lila stuck out on her team too, not because she was a prude or a giantess, but because... because...

I didn't really have an answer for that. She just *did*. Or at least she did to me. Ever since I first saw her and offered to have a catch with her because her team had an odd number of players, I thought there was something different about her. She was cool. She was funny.

And a new sparkling little thought entered my brain that hadn't been there before. Or at the very least, hadn't let itself become part of my waking consciousness before.

She was sexy too.

There was no use denying it. It would be like denying the sky was blue. I found Lila sexy. I had to sit with that and let it simmer, because it meant a whole lot of things were about to change. I wasn't going to be able to interact with her the way I had before, for one thing. Star was, for all intents and purposes, my girlfriend. The fact that we really hadn't done much beyond a single makeout session was beside the point. I had an expectation that we were together, so I had to act accordingly.

That meant not tempting myself.

But how was I going to do that without it being obvious? And was I really going to be able to do it at all? Lila was the only person on this trip other than Kevin that I had any interest in hanging out with. Plus, she was sick, and I wanted to make sure she felt better. She was my friend, regardless of how I realized I felt about her now. Avoiding her would be a dick move.

I stayed staring at the ceiling, tossing it all through my mind over and over. Eventually, I decided I wasn't going to decide anything tonight. It wasn't going to be resolved before the sun rose, and I had a big day tomorrow. I needed the sleep.

Forcing my eyes closed and focusing on my breathing, I let the soft whisper of the video on my phone lull me into loosely connected and weird dreams. But eventually, I slept.

# Chapter Two

## *Lila*

FOR A WHILE, I DREAMED.

I was adrift on the sea, curled on my side on a small raft. But I wasn't afraid. I was comfortable, breathing in the salty air and enjoying the warmth of the sun on my skin. I was naked, and though I loosely worried about the sunburn I would have, suffering from the wrath of the ancient curse of my ancestors, it wasn't my primary concern. In fact, nothing was. I didn't have any concerns.

My head rested on an arm. Strong, muscular and protective, the arm held my head aloft better than any pillow. It made me feel safe.

Then the rest of the body attached to that arm curled around me. Another arm draped over my hip and settled on my stomach. Fingers traced my belly button, and I stretched my legs down until my toes brushed over the body's shins. I let one leg rest on top of them, parting my thighs just so.

Fingers slid up my body and filled with one breast as I let my head fall back. Kisses began to press against my shoulder as my nipples hardened. Then the hand slid down, down, down. Down between my thighs until it touched me and made me gasp. My own hand slid behind me and filled with the warm, soft skin of a hardened cock. I stroked it and heard a groan. I smiled.

I rolled on my back to give the body greater access. The face came into view.

It was Gavin.

And I awoke.

The lights were off, and for a moment I was completely lost. I had no idea where I was, what time of the night it was, anything. I was so sure there had been someone in the bed with me, but now it was empty. Just me. In the darkness.

Then pieces of the night before began to slide into place. A glass on the nightstand that I didn't remember putting there. The sheets on the other side of the bed were folded over, like someone had gotten out of it.

Gavin. Like Gavin had gotten out of it.

Was that real? Was he really there, or had I just had some crazy fever dream? Had he really been in my bed with me?

My eyes floated over to the table and the tiny loveseat across from it. A bag sat on the table, turned on its side. Candies and games spilled out of it. A cup with dice inside and several sheets of paper, dark scribble lines visible in the soft light of the parking lot light outside my window.

He had been here. Gavin had been in my room all night and had helped take care of me. It was starting to come back now. We'd played dice for what seemed like hours, keeping score on his weird but fun game and getting probably a little too loud when we rolled big numbers.

Then we had lain down, and I had listened to his heartbeat with my head on his chest while we watched something on the phone. And I fell asleep. I could have sworn he did too.

At some point, he'd slipped out of the room. He must have been extremely quiet, because even sick, I was a pretty light sleeper. I would figure I would have heard him when he opened and shut the door. But the room was empty aside from me.

I wondered if he was embarrassed to be there. With me. It would explain why he didn't wake me when he left. If he was so ashamed to have fallen asleep with me, in the bed no less, then I could see him sneaking out under the cover of darkness. He probably wouldn't ever even speak of it again, or worse, avoid me.

Visions of how awkward the rest of the week would be were dancing through my mind. I didn't really realize until that moment how much I had depended on hanging out with Gavin to make the week better. Sure, the tournaments and practices were going to take up most of my time, but I had looked forward to hanging out with Gavin and Star all the way up until Star decided not to come. But without her, I still had this hope that Gavin and I would keep each other company, even if it meant hanging around mostly other baseball players and dealing with the inevitable bad jokes and frat boy humor of some of them.

Then again, he had come over to spend a lot of time last night just to take care of me. All because I was sick. Someone who would do that wouldn't just up and ghost me for the rest of the week. He would at least check in and make sure I was feeling better, right? I had to believe he was the kind of guy that if something did make him feel uncomfortable, he would either want to talk about it or would just ignore it happened, rather than let it affect our friendship negatively.

At any rate, I felt a lot better than I had. Normally when I woke up, I felt dizzy and exhausted, like someone had put me in one of those gravity rides at the fair, the ones that spun you around and around and you stuck to the walls as they rose up and down. I could never handle those things. They always made me sick.

My stomach didn't feel like I had spun around for three minutes after eating pretzel dogs, so that was something in the win column at least. I tried to shake off the disappointment that Gavin was gone and the worry that I had somehow offended him. He had been so comfortable to curl up with. I envied that Star had that whenever she wanted, and a part of me despised that she'd so easily given it up to go off with her other friends in Europe.

If he had been dating me, I would never leave the room. Not when he was in it.

Slowly, my eyes began to shut again, and I curled back up on the pillows, tucking one into my chest and draping my arm over it. It was a poor replacement for Gavin's thick, muscular chest, but it was something. I sighed and felt sleep begin to take over my consciousness again. One more nap wouldn't kill me. It would probably help, actually. Besides, the sun wasn't up yet. I had some time.

I tried to focus on a happy thought. Something to guide my mind into pleasant dreams. I thought about the games I was to play later, envisioning myself winning. How the trophy would feel in my hands as I hoisted it before handing it to the next girl in line after our win. How sweet the last meal of the trip would be, some big thing our whole team would do, as we tasted not just the food but the sweet nectar of victory. Of how happy Gavin would be for me when I told him we won. How he would hug me, squeezing me tight and congratulating me.

How his hug would linger.

How we would go back to my room, celebrating and laughing. How our hands would fill with each other's and cling tightly as we walked the halls of the hotel. How we would find ourselves alone in the hall, in the restaurant, in the room. How he would kiss me.

I could nearly feel his fingertips brushing up my hip, pulling at my shirt until it untucked. I would still be in my uniform, still sweaty from the game. But so would he. He still had the eyeblack on, smeared over his cheek like a warrior. My hat would fly off of me as he tore my shirt over my head. We would kiss, and he would pick me up, carrying me to the bathroom, where I would spin the faucet and turn on the shower.

We would climb inside, still clothed and giggling. I would tear at his pants until the bulge inside revealed itself to be a long, thick, warm cock. I would stroke it and kiss up his chest until he spun me against the wall. I would gasp as he picked up my leg, holding it aloft as he thrust his massive member deep inside me, and I would cry out in ecstasy.

Our clothes would be piled on the bottom of the shower, dirt swirling down the drain from sliding into bases and diving for catches. As we washed ourselves under the water, he would spin me so my back was to him and fill his hand with my braids. He would fuck me with abandon, and I would let my finger slide down between my thighs. Just the slightest touch on my clit would send me over the edge and have me tumbling into an incredible climax.

I would shout his name.

Just a touch...

My eyes snapped open. My hand was on my thigh, so close to the throbbing center that begged for release. The sun was still not up yet, but the sky had turned dark blue, light brightening it up and making the deep purple of night retreat westward.

I was sweating, the sheets soaked. At war with myself, I forcibly removed my own hand from my body and flopped over onto my stomach. What was I doing? I couldn't think about him this way. He was Star's boyfriend. My best friend's boyfriend. I should be ashamed of myself.

And I was. Enough that I peeled myself out of the bed and made my way to the bathroom. I turned on the water, nice and cool, and stepped inside. It was jarring to have a shower that wasn't blazing hot, but I needed it. I needed to not be comfortable and let my mind wander again. Once I felt like the sweat was gone and I smelled like the flowery soap I had brought from home, I stepped out and quickly dressed. I didn't want to be naked. It was too much of a temptation.

I was wide awake. The shower helped, but the vision, no, fantasy that I had been having about Gavin was what really did it. It had been so real. So visceral. I had never had such an intense dream about another man. Certainly not one that was real. That I could reach out and touch. Or that I had spent a considerable amount of time sleeping in the same bed as.

I could still smell him on the sheets. His cologne. His sweat.

Pulling the sheets off the bed, I crumpled them by the door. I would ask for new ones when I left for practice later. Then that temptation would be gone too.

I went over to the little coffee maker and set it to brew a cup. It was one of those single-serve pod things, and I was grateful for the ease of use of it. I preferred good coffee, from fresh beans, but this would do. As it brewed, I turned on the television, keeping it low so I didn't disturb Sara in the door next to mine.

Sitting on the couch, I looked out over the beach from the angle I could see. I mostly saw the parking lot, but I got a little bit of the ocean too. The sun was coming up fast, a thin line of near white at the edge of the horizon. It wouldn't be long until everyone else was awake and moving around too.

Pulling the cards out of the bag, I turned on the light next to me and listened to the weather channel as I dealt the cards. A little game of solitaire to pass the time. After a little while, I realized my phone was dead and went to go put it on the charger. It would have to boot up again. I had run it completely dead watching whatever Gavin and I had watched as we fell asleep.

Part of me wished I could go back in time, just for a few more minutes. If I could just relive the night.

I might not have slept.

# Chapter Three

## *Gavin*

THIS WAS GETTING RIDICULOUS.

I could see the color of the sky changing, going from the inky, purple darkness to a dark blue. It wouldn't be long before there was white in the sky and my alarm would go off. Then I had to get up, get a quick workout in, drink my protein shake, and get ready for the day.

None of which I wanted to do.

As much as I loved playing baseball, right now, all I wanted to do was lie there and try to figure myself out. There was so much going on in my head, and I couldn't make sense of it. None of it was going to be easy to work through. And it all compounded on each other.

My family life was a mess, but that wasn't new. I'd compartmentalized that a long time ago. But the worry that Dad was in some kind of real trouble this time was enough to make me think about it once in a while. I often wondered if his bad decisions would end up affecting me in some way beyond being annoying. If some scout would see my family problems as a liability and not sign me. Something like that.

But I couldn't concentrate on an abstract like that right now. Not when there was a very real, very present problem going on. One that was driving me absolutely crazy.

I couldn't stop thinking about Lila.

It was ridiculous. I had practice in a few hours, and I was going to need to be at my top form for this tournament. I needed the rest. So why was my brain not letting go of what happened tonight and all the complicated feelings it brought up? It was confusing. It was aggravating.

It was intoxicating.

Something about Lila had gotten way down deep under my skin. At first, she had been just a friend, a cute one, sure, but a friend. A friend I could talk about baseball with, and then one I was mentoring to get through her classes. We chatted about movies and TV and silly shit. Nothing serious. Nothing that would lead to a relationship beyond friendship. Just mutual fun talk.

But as time went on, I found myself thinking about her more and more. Enough that it intruded on other thoughts. Thoughts that I didn't want them intruding on. Thoughts about Star.

At first, I was able to brush it off as an anomaly. I hadn't been with anyone in a while, and Star was being rather more patient than I expected her to be. Not that it bothered me; it was just a surprise. I got the impression from her and how handsy she seemed to be with her artsy friends that physical intimacy was no big deal for her. That if she were in a relationship, a major element would be the physicality.

Yet, none of that had manifested. Which, originally, I was actually kind of pleased with. I liked the idea of getting to know her as a person. About our relationship being more than sex and lust. I thought she was fascinating and funny and weird in the best ways. But after a while, I was still surprised she hadn't shown much interest beyond kissing.

Then again, I hadn't really pushed it either. Why was that? Why hadn't I just gone for it? Why hadn't I slid my hand under her shirt during one of our rare makeout sessions on the couch? Done something to signal that I wanted to take things to the bedroom?

It always seemed like if that thought did come through my mind, something stopped it. Either it was getting late and I needed to be at my place to get my stuff for the morning, or Star had some project to do. Or the knowledge that Lila was in the next room, her door shut, but her light on. She was awake. I didn't want her to hear us.

But why? When had that ever stopped me?

It was a lot to think about, and I had shoved it all into the corners of my mind until now. With everything that happened tonight, though, it was all spilling out. Threatening to take over every inch of my thought. To force me to deal with it.

I pressed my eyes shut hard. I had to get the thoughts away and onto something that I could let myself relax with. I tried to think about baseball.

If I had a lefty at the plate, and he had a high zone and ate cutters for breakfast, how would I get him out if he got ahead in the count? Sliders are too much like cutters, just slower. My sinker was good, but you have to set that up with something, and cutter hitting lefties usually see a right-handed change-up coming a mile away. A splitter? Too much like the sink. A curve? It'd have to be the curve. Not twelve-six though, something with an angle. Something with some funk.

My eyes opened, and I groaned. I was no closer to sleeping. And that scenario had been the extent of my ability to distract myself. I didn't even want to think about baseball anymore.

The only comfort I got was thinking about how comfortable I had been in the bed with Lila. Maybe if I put myself in exactly the same position, it could trigger something. Flailing around for a minute, I finally remembered I had my right hand behind my head, one pillow underneath me to support my neck. The other pillow that had propped me up so I could see the phone had slid under my right shoulder, so I put one there. One leg was turned into the knee of the other, making a figure four.

The only thing missing was Lila.

The weight of her head on my shoulder, slowly drifting to my chest and fitting so perfectly. It had been calming and exciting at the same time in a way I couldn't even explain to myself. Her breast had been pressed against my ribs, and I could tell she wasn't wearing a bra under the hoodie she had pulled over her. Why would she? She had been sick.

I wondered how that breast felt outside of that hoodie. How soft and full it would have felt in my hand. How sweet her lips must be. How fantastic her ass had looked in her softball uniform, and how nice it would be to slide my hands over it, to let my fingers dip between her cheeks and inch toward the warm center of her body.

"Stop it," I said to myself. "Stop."

I tried to shake it off and think solely about how easily I fell asleep before. What had it been that made it so easy to rest? I needed to get back to that. I needed some sleep before the game.

I started to settle as I thought about how comfortable I had been with her in my arm. I tried to let my mind float into a fantasy, but doing a little extra work. Replacing Lila with Star. Imagining what should have been.

In my vision, Star would be draped over me just like Lila had been. Her blond hair fell over her face as she snuggled into my chest. My cock started to thicken again as I imagined her rolling all the way on top of me, kissing my neck and working her way down. Her hair still covered her face in the way she let it sometimes when she slept on the couch as she tore at my shorts.

I closed my eyes as I let the fantasy fill my mind. One hand slipped down to my cock and pulled it out of the shorts as in my fantasy, her hand began to do the work. I would reach up and slide my hand under her hoodie, pulling it up over her soft, round breasts. They would tumble out in my hand as she released me and yanked on the hoodie herself. It was almost over her head now, pushing her hair back behind her so all my fantasy could see was the hoodie over her head and her exposed chest.

I stroked faster and faster, moaning in the bed as I grew as hard as I had been in a long time.

The hoodie would be pulled all the way up. As it was tossed to the floor, she would yank her head back, letting her brown locks fall behind her.

It wasn't Star anymore. It was Lila.

And it was too late to stop.

I would pull her toward me, and our lips would crush into each other. While we kissed, she would be pulling down on the uniform pants she was suddenly wearing. She would kick them off, and they would pile onto the corner of the bed. She would crawl onto her side, kissing my chest on the way down as she lay so she could see into my eyes.

She would smile as she reached my cock and slipped it between her lips.

I would groan and let my hand slide down her body until it reached her center. She would be wearing red, lacy panties, and I would slide my fingers inside. She would already be wet, hot, and waiting. She would move her legs so one was propped up and gave me greater access while she stroked me onto her tongue.

I wouldn't be able to hold myself much longer, and I would swirl my finger over her clit before pushing it deep inside her. She would gasp and moan over my cock, and I would respond in kind. The adrenaline would take over. The need for her, the need for release, the need to claim.

I would pull her over and yank the panties off of her, diving my face between her thighs as she straddled me. My tongue would slide through her folds, and her body would quiver as I brought her to climax. I would squeeze her ass as she came and then begged for me to be inside her.

Rolling her to her back, I would mount her, pulling her legs up and around my waist as I stared deep into her eyes. She wanted me. She wanted me inside her.

I rolled onto my side in the bed, my cock about to explode as I kept my eyes clenched in the fantasy. I pressed my heels into the mattress and arched up as I neared climax myself. And in my vision, I slammed into her.

She would be crying out my name between whimpers. A guttural roar would build in my chest, and her eyes would open wide as she came again. I would be so close, and she could feel it. She wanted it. She wanted my come.

She would beg for it.

Inside her.

My hands would clench over her hips as I slammed into her over and over. And finally, when our voices made harmony and our bodies arched as one, I would explode into her.

In my hand, I squeezed as my essence spilled out, covering the sheet on one side until I was empty. Crumpled in exhaustion and exertion, I reached blindly for the tissues on the nightstand. I would have to leave my sheets to be cleaned. But for now, I was finally tired. Finally feeling like I could sleep.

In the warmth of the glow of my fantasy, with visions of her naked body curled against me in a deep, grinning sleep, I let my body relax into the pillows on the other side of the bed. Slowly, my eyes closed fully, and my breathing slowed. My heart returned to normal.

And I slept. Dreaming of Lila. Kissing her in my sleep, cupping her breast as I held her close, listening to her heart as she dreamed.

# Chapter Four

## *Lila*

A KNOCKING ON MY DOOR startled me out of sleep and into a state of complete confusion.

Why was I on the couch, curled up like I was napping at home, when I was clearly in a hotel? What time was it? Why hadn't my alarm gone off to wake me up? Who the hell was knocking on my door?

Where was Gavin?

That last one got to me, and the rest of the night whooshed into my memory like a freight train. Suddenly, I remembered why I had ended up on the couch playing the saddest game of solitaire I had ever played. I remembered my eyes getting heavy as the sun rose and turning the television down so it was barely above a whisper. How I pulled the hoodie up and over my eyes so I couldn't see the light streaming in from the window.

And how I had wished Gavin had stayed the entire night. And how I wasn't sure I could have trusted myself if he had.

The knocks paused for a few moments and then started again. They were light, like someone was simultaneously trying to wake me up and let me sleep. It had the effect of someone very gently tapping out the drum part for a rock song instead.

"Just a second," I said.

No voice greeted me from the other side, and a sudden thought entered my mind. What if that was Gavin out there? It would make sense for him to come check on me, as much as I had convinced myself that he was going to try to avoid me the rest of the week.

Stumbling to my feet, I wondered if I looked even remotely presentable. I mean, he saw me last night, right? I had to look worse then. I certainly felt worse then. I could probably go play today if I wanted to push myself.

One step toward the door threw that thought into serious question.

The woozy walk to the door was peppered with flails at my hair and an attempt to make myself look like I wasn't a hideous troll monster, all while doing everything I could to convince myself that I was only doing that out of vanity and totally not because I wanted to look good specifically because it might be Gavin on the other side of the door.

I took a deep breath and turned the handle, trying out a smile to see if it made a difference. When the door revealed a very dressed, very perky Sara on the other side, I knew I faltered a little, but not enough that her face should be scrunching up like that. Or make her take a half step back.

"Oh, babe, you look like shit," Sara said, her thick New York accent cutting through the bullshit of Southern Charm and getting right to the point.

"Thanks," I said, letting the rest of my façade smile melt away into nothingness.

"I mean, I'm sorry, you just look terrible," she said, not helping matters at all, but looking like she thought she had. "I came to check on you and see if you were coming to practice, but, uhh..."

"I guess I don't look like it, huh?" I asked.

She shook her head slowly.

"I didn't mean to wake you up. I just figured if you *were* up, I'd be able to chat with you. Um. So, I'll just tell Coach you'll take today off?"

"I suppose," I said. "I mean, I could probably push it..."

"Nah," she said, waving me off with her catcher's mitt-sized hand. For such a short girl, Sara had awfully big hands, which one would think would make her an ideal backstop. Instead, she was dead-set on playing shortstop, and somehow made it work. "I'll tell Coach I saw you and I know for a fact you ain't faking it."

"I appreciate it," I said, wondering if she could recognize the deadness of my voice and realizing she, much like Star, was completely oblivious to it.

"Cool. So just get some rest, okay? We need you for the games."

"Will do," I said, closing the door slowly.

As the door clicked shut, I shook my head.

I felt good enough to play, but it was probably for the best for me to rest. I didn't sleep much, that was for sure, and usually when I felt fine after being sick, it tended to mean I still needed a day of taking it easy before I was at a hundred percent. Otherwise, I might make myself sick again.

My head felt like it was full of mush, too. The dizziness had gone away once I got moving, but I didn't really feel like I could think straight. Part of it was the frustration that every time I let myself zone out at all, my mind went to Gavin and then to how absolutely, infuriatingly stupid it was to do that. But it had felt so natural falling asleep on his shoulder. I couldn't get over how natural it felt.

How right.

Enough was enough. I needed to nip this in the bud and bring a cold dash of water to my perspective. I needed to just get into contact with Star and let my own over-developed sense of guilt drive the thoughts of Gavin out of my mind.

Also, another shower would probably be good. Something warmer this time and soothing. Something I could take my time in and really enjoy. And get my hair clean.

One of the great mysteries of the morning was solved when I went to pick my phone up from the charger. It had stayed turned off, power charging through the night. It meant my alarm never sounded, but at least it was at full power.

Turning it on, I waited for the apps to boot up before I pulled open my texts. I almost expected to see a couple of new ones once it generated, one from Star checking in and maybe one from Gavin. I wondered which one I would click first if they were both there. My brain wanted to say Star, but I had my doubts.

But when the messages loaded, there was nothing new. I even pulled down to refresh the screen and nothing popped up. Not even spam messages.

I opened up Star's messages and paused before I typed. What exactly was I going to say? That I technically, but totally not in the way you think, slept with your boyfriend last night? Or would it be better to just say I cuddled her boyfriend most of the night? Neither of those sounded like they would go over very well and would probably be misinterpreted rather quickly. Even by Star, who generally didn't care to read the lines, much less what was between them.

Instead, I just texted her a good morning message. Something to get the conversation going. I could eventually laugh my way into a conversation with her that began with 'You're going to think this is funny, just wait until the end. Last night...'

I waited expectantly for a few minutes, and then realized the time difference probably meant she was busy. It would be almost three in the afternoon there, and if her routine in Georgia was any indication, Star was likely having a long lunch and drawing something about right now. I shrugged and put the phone down on the bed. Technically it was the kind of phone that was supposed to be able to get wet, but I didn't trust that. I'd rather it stay in another room entirely.

As I started the shower, I let my hair down and made sure I had the shampoo and conditioner from home in the tub. I let the water get nice and hot before I stepped in and took a few deep breaths as I adjusted to it. I got my hair wet first, and immediately put in shampoo so I felt accomplished.

But as the shampoo rolled down my neck and over my collarbones, I felt my body coming alive. My thoughts raced, and suddenly I found myself zoning out again, blankly staring at the wall as one hand moved up my side toward my nipple, soap dangling precariously off the hardened tip, while the other began to move down and in toward my center.

Nope. Nope, nope, nope. Not doing that. Not when I was literally waiting on Star to text me back.

I rinsed the shampoo out of my hair, mumbling at myself in frustration. I tried to let my mind think of something else. Anything. Softball. Trigonometry. Bob Newhart. *Something.*

I put the conditioner on my hair and stepped out of the direct line of water enough to not rinse it out immediately, turning my chest toward the beating shower. It was one of the upsides of this hotel, for sure. The hotel's water pressure was fantastic.

Maybe I could turn today into one of those days like when I was in elementary school and randomly got a day off. I could run down to the lobby and get a bowl of cereal and bring it up to my room. I could watch *The Price is Right* and check out a bunch of sub-Reddits that I had been meaning to fall down the rabbit hole of. I could make the day something fun, nap a bunch, and by the time tomorrow came, I'd be ready to put my fingers across the seam of a softball and fire it over the plate.

A ding went off in the bedroom, and I nearly fell out of the shower trying to get out. I was mutually excited about the prospect that Gavin could be texting me as I was that Star had responded. Maybe I should wrap a towel around myself. In case it was Gavin.

What a silly thought. It wasn't like he could see me.

But I would know. I would know I was naked, wet, and dripping while looking at words he wrote me.

Oh, dammit all to hell, I needed to get over it already.

Picking up the phone, I swiped up and saw that the message was actually from Star. Breathing a sigh of relief, mixed with disappointment, I opened it up. Then I got weirdly angry.

It was a picture.

Star, standing in the center of the frame, clearly holding the phone out to take the selfie, was wearing a bikini. A rather tiny one by the looks of it, but that was Star. She was either in a full, weird hippie dress or barely any clothes at all. But that wasn't what bothered me.

It was the three other people in the photo. One girl, who I recognized as one of Star's long-time friends, and two boys. Neither of them looked familiar, but they both looked like they did *a lot* of crunches. They were the skinny type, a type I had never found very attractive but Star had gone for before. The loose, finely curated 'I don't care' look of their hair, swooping down over one eye as if they just simply didn't need depth perception. The shorts hung low to show off a 'v' shape on their washboard stomachs. Spindly legs that looked like they had never been used to lift anything more than the weight of a video game controller or a surfboard, in that order.

They were her type.

And she was clearly having fun with them.

I was jealous on Gavin's behalf, and it was really weird. Especially considering that he had no room to talk, having spent the night in another girl's hotel room.

Frustrated, and completely confused as to how to feel, I took the phone with me into the bathroom but left the door open. I needed to get the conditioner out, and I decided that no one would mind if I blasted music since everyone on the floor was at practice by now. Turning the volume up, I stepped back in the shower and started rinsing out my hair, trying desperately not to think about Gavin or Star.

# Chapter Five

## *Gavin*

THE PHONE WAS RINGING.

Why was the phone ringing?

It was ringing a lot. Like someone was really desperate to get ahold of me.

I let it ring without opening my eyes. If it was important, they would call bac...

They called back.

Immediately.

Dammit.

I opened my eyes and was confused for just a moment when I didn't see my apartment. Then it hit me in a rush, and adrenaline got dumped directly into my heart.

I shot up, snatching at the phone and rubbing my eyes as I put the receiver end to my ear.

"Hello?"

"Gavin, where the fuck are you, bud?"

It was Kevin. Of course it was Kevin. He would be the one to check on me before anyone else. As much as I hated to admit it, I was a star. If I felt like skipping a practice, no one else on the team would have the balls to say anything about it other than Kevin. And he would give me shit about it unless I had a good reason.

"Shit," I said. "Shit, what time is it?"

"Dude, it's like nine," Kevin said. "We've been on the field for a half hour now. I thought you were just doing a protein shake breakfast and some crunches or something. Were you still in bed?"

"Sort of," I said, tossing the sheet off of me and realizing I was still naked. And the reason why I was still naked.

"Did you go out last night?" Kevin asked. "I only ask because one of the guys swears he saw you, but I thought you were going to go check up on Lila and then hit the hay early."

"I did. Kind of," I said. "It's a whole story."

"Yeah, he said you saw Star," Kevin said, letting the words sit heavily in the silence.

"I did?" I said. "I don't remember saying that."

"Right, right," Kevin said. "'Cuz she's not in town. So you couldn't have seen her. But he said you looked right drunk, so..."

"I'll tell you, Kev, I'm a little shaky on the details of last night."

Technically, that was the truth. I was a little shaky on the details. But they just weren't the kinds of details he was thinking they were.

I hated deceiving Kevin. I was probably going to tell him the whole story once I got him alone, but for now, I knew everything I was saying was getting back to Coach and the boys. For some reason, I had a feeling me going out and drinking like the rest of them would go over better than me staying in one of the girls' rooms all night.

"Well, Coach said if you need the morning off to take it. But the rest of the boys are here, and every last damn one of them have hangovers. Raul puked at second base. Asian Dan is asleep on the bench. Even Coach looks a bit out of it, to be fair."

"I don't need the morning off," I said. "I'll get a shake in and head down in a few minutes."

"Cool. See you then," he said.

As the phone clicked, I tossed it beside me on the bed and put my head in my hands. At least my tiredness would apparently fit in with the rest of the boys' hangovers. I might even be able to pull the story off.

I made my shake and guzzled it down as I got my uniform on, then drank a bottle of water to chase it. Usually, I would have a coffee too, but I didn't have the time this morning. With my uniform on, I grabbed my phone and my bat bag and headed out of the door. I was tempted to drop by Lila's room and see if she was all right, but then I would have to address how everything went last night. I wasn't quite ready for that.

When I was ready, I still didn't know what I would say. 'Hey, sorry I fell asleep in your bed and then left in the middle of the night because I already have a girlfriend, your roommate'? That didn't exactly slide off the tongue, and no matter how I framed it, it still sounded kind of accusatory and rude.

I had to shake it off and get to playing baseball. That was what I was good at. A bit of toss and some batting practice should take my mind off Lila. And Star. But mostly Lila.

As I reached the field, just down the street from the hotel, I could see what Kevin had been talking about.

Kevin was a huge fire hydrant, dressed in the red uniform of our away clothes and standing amidst the rest of the team. They weren't in position, just casually tossing, which meant either they hadn't really started all that long ago, or Coach had given up on anything much more complex than that given the state of the players.

I caught Kevin's attention as I got into the cage where our bench was and he jogged over. He had a ball in one hand and a grin on his face.

"Ready?" he asked, his deep, tree-trunk voice still sounding much like the little kid I'd gotten to know when we met.

"Guess so," I said, flipping my hat back around the right way.

"No shades?" he asked.

"What?" I asked.

It was a gray morning, clouds covering most of the sky and a little bit of darkness threatening off in the horizon. Whether that was real or just the weather anomaly of being near the ocean and having ever-changing patterns I didn't know. But despite the dimness of the light, as I looked around, I could see that virtually every member of the team besides Kevin was wearing sunglasses.

They were also moving like their bodies were trapped in molasses and throwing like their arms were made of gelatin.

"Shades," Kevin said. "You must not have gotten as fucked up as everyone else. Good for you. Not quite as good as my ten p.m. special, but I'm sure you had fun."

"I did," I said, leaving it at that.

"Well, come on, let's go warm up, and you can regale me with tales of bikini-clad girls and copious amounts of alcohol."

"It really wasn't like th—" I began.

"Regale me," Kevin said, already walking off toward right field.

Shrugging, I jogged after him, but slowly to continue the illusion of a hangover.

Kevin, as usual, stopped at the foul line, meaning I was the one expected to take the jog closer to center field. Kevin was wildly athletic despite his size and could easily roam around the outfield, but he was keenly aware of his knees. Being a catcher, he didn't particularly like running much outside of his workouts designed to strengthen the muscles around his knees. If he was going to make it long as a catcher, he needed to preserve them as much as possible.

I jogged out a bit and turned to see a ball already leaving his hand. Kevin also had a rocket for an arm, though his accuracy was a little suspect sometimes. If he was firing from the plate to second base, he was like a laser. But without the specific layout of the infield, sometimes his tosses sliced a bit one direction or the other. I chased down the first throw a few steps away to my right and tossed it back mid-stride.

We warmed up for a while, slowly losing other members of the team as they headed back toward the bench and started working out batting practice order. When it was just the two of us, Kevin looked back toward the bench and then back to me before tossing a throw.

"So you fixin' to tell me what happened last night?"

"I told you, it's shaky," I began.

"Bullshit. I know fake drunk when I see it," he said. "I do enough of it myself just to keep people from continuing to challenge me at shots."

I nodded. Kevin's alcohol consumption ability was legendary, as was his apparent dislike of proving it. He would party occasionally, but often preferred a glass of wine and an early night instead. I had witnessed him winking at me, completely sober, before donning a very convincing act as a drunken giant. I would help him away from whatever crowd we were with, and he would revert back to soberness as soon as we were out of their vision and drive us back home.

"I went and made sure Lila was good, and then I spent the rest of the night doing what I wanted," I said. "Where's the crime?"

Kevin smirked. "No crime, per se," he said. "I just doubt you got hammered and fucked around behind Star's back."

"All right, you got me," I said, feeling warmth crawl up my neck. I wasn't entirely sure I could deny fucking around on Star behind her back. I didn't *do* anything with Lila. But what we had done was probably not okay, and I certainly went a few extra steps in my fantasy a little later, for which I felt terribly guilty.

"Spill it, boss," Kevin said.

"I didn't get drunk, and I didn't find a girl at the beach, all right? I just kind of spent some time out of my room, watched a bunch of shows on my phone, and fell asleep. When I got back in, everyone was drunk and just assumed I was too, so I went with it. It was easier and less embarrassing than the truth."

"Fair," Kevin said. "Though, you should know, you could probably get away with that without hazing while the rest of us couldn't. Hell, it might even make Coach like you *more* that you didn't get drunk and took a nap instead."

I shrugged.

"So, wait, how did you end up sleeping in?" he asked.

"Forgot to charge my phone," I said. "No alarm this morning."

It was a complete lie, but Kevin bought it. I hated myself for lying to him, but it was the only thing I could do that didn't expose Lila. Until I knew how she felt about last night, I didn't want anyone else knowing about it.

"Well, looks like we're going to do a bit of batting practice," Kevin said. "You down for that?"

"Sure," I said. "Let's go."

Seemingly satisfied for now, but with the faintest hint of suspicion in his eyes, Kevin nodded, and we jogged back to the bench to put away our gloves and grab a bat.

A few hours later, practice ended early, and Kevin went back to the room before I did. He was planning on ordering room service and watching a movie and had invited me to join him if I wanted. A couple of the other guys were going to come over, and the only rule was no alcohol. It was a sodas and water only event.

I headed back at my own pace, slowing as I passed the field where the girls were still practicing. Noticeably fewer of them had sunglasses on and the tell-tale lethargic shuffle of a hangover. Yet, among them, I didn't see Lila. I wondered if I should drop by her room again and decided I would at least go back to my room and get cleaned up before I did, if I did at all.

As I crested the last of the steps to my floor, I felt a tingling sensation in the back of my head. It was one of those weird things that happen when you're sure someone is talking about you. I wondered if Lila was telling someone about last night. If she was, I could come clean to Kevin too. But that would most certainly mean talking to Star.

Mulling that over in my mind, I made my way to my room and stopped a few feet away from it.

There was a note on the door. A yellow sticky note with dark writing.

At first, my heart clenched in a strange way at the thought it could be Lila. But as I got closer, I recognized the handwriting. It wasn't Lila's. It wasn't Star's either.

It was Mom's.

# Chapter Six

## *Lila*

AROUND TWO, EMMA CAME to check on me, bringing me a couple bottles of water and an orange juice. Thirty or so minutes later, Amanda came by with a sandwich and some gossip about what Emma had been up to last night. Apparently, a group of the girls had gone to the pool rather early and met up with a couple of boys that weren't with the baseball team. Not long after, Emma had disappeared for several hours, and when she returned was blushing, giggling, and wearing a T-shirt that looked suspiciously large on her.

While I wasn't one much for gossip, it made me feel good to have them both check in on me to try to help keep me feeling included. Sometimes I wondered if I really fit in with them beyond the game, but days like this helped. At least I was cared about.

Weirdly, though, as the day went on and bled into the early evening, I still hadn't heard from Gavin. Not even a text at this point. I wondered if he just felt weird about the whole situation and was avoiding me, or if he was just busy. I hadn't seen the boys running around yet, so it was possible they were just having a long practice and Gavin hadn't gotten free yet.

I was feeling a lot better, enough that I felt like maybe not wearing pajamas for a little while. I knew it was primarily a mental thing, but if I put on *actual clothes*, maybe I wouldn't fall back into feeling like absolute crud when the sun went fully down.

The suitcase was a mess. I hadn't really bothered to unpack since I had been sick on arrival and had instead just yanked things out of it at random when I needed them. Sighing, I started putting things away in the drawers, keeping out a pair of shorts and a T-shirt that I wanted to change into when I got done.

"Hot damn, Lila, did you bring anything other than pajamas?" I muttered to myself.

I had six shirts, two pairs of shorts, one pair of jeans, a dress, and a myriad of socks. The rest of the suitcase was either panties or pajamas. A lot of pajamas. Apparently, I was already thinking about getting rest when I was packing.

Shaking my head, I put everything away, then made my way to the bathroom to change. Strictly speaking, I had no reason for modesty. It was my room, and no one could just barge in. But years of intrusive parents who let me have almost no private space without locking doors and being prepared to yell if I heard jiggling on the handle left me wanting to double up on my privacy.

I caught sight of myself in the mirror as I changed shirts. For a tiny moment, I wondered what Gavin would say if he saw me like this. If he had happened to walk into my room and caught me just like this. Then I shook my head and tried to push those thoughts away. I knew how he would react. He would leave, embarrassed, and then make fun of me for it.

Because he was my friend. Nothing more.

Once changed, I went back into my room and tooled around on my phone for a bit while the television played local weather. As expected, it was supposed to be wonderful all week, perfect for sunbathing and playing baseball.

The hotel seemed much quieter than the night before. There weren't tons of voices or people padding up and down the hallway like there had been. Apparently, everyone had gotten their partying out of their system, at least for now. The silence likely wouldn't last all the way to the end of the week.

I found myself flipping back to my messenger app, convinced that if I refreshed it, a new message would show up. One from Gavin, probably complaining about Star and how dumb she was being. Or checking in on me. Or talking about baseball. Something.

But nothing had come in yet, and it was starting to bug me. A lot. Enough that finally, I decided I needed to do something about it or I would spend the rest of the night worrying about it. I needed to make sure he was cool and our friendship was still fine.

Putting on socks but not bothering with shoes, I grabbed my door key card and stuffed it in my bra. The gym shorts were sans-pockets, one of the many issues I tended to have with clothes in general. There were never enough pockets. At least for my clothes. Guys seemed to have pockets to spare.

Slipping out of my room, I waited to see if there was going to be company, anyone to question me as to where I was going. When no one came out of their door, jogging over to pepper me with questions like an old-timey reporter in a Superman movie, I went to the stairwell and went up the flight of stairs to the boys' floor.

Perhaps I overestimated how good I felt, because as I reached the top step, I had to stop for a moment. *By tomorrow, I should feel normal,* I told myself, *but today, maybe I use elevators.*

I opened the door to the boys' floor, noting that it was as quiet as the one below. The boys were apparently working out their own hangovers alone in their rooms too. Part of me felt like I had missed out a bit on the fun, but at the same time, if I had the choice of partying with Emma or hanging out with Gavin...

Gavin had kind of told me which room he was in when he came over, saying it was directly above mine and one over, so I went to the door to the left of the one above me and let out a breath. If it wasn't his room, then it meant he was in the one on the other side. But if it wasn't his room and someone answered, it would let some of his teammates know I was coming to his room, so I kind of hoped I was making the right guess.

I knocked.

There was silence on the other side.

I waited a moment and knocked again, thinking that if no one answered, maybe I should try the door on the other side. Maybe the person inside this one who wasn't Gavin took a look through the peephole, saw the sick girl from the softball team, and decided to leave me waiting.

I was about to give up and move to the next room when the door beside me opened. Kevin's head popped out, looking left and then right at me. I smiled, and his giant bear grin took up his whole face.

"Well, hey there, Lila," he said. "Looks like you're feeling a bit better."

"I am," I said. "Last couple of days have kicked my ass, but I'm finally feeling a bit more like a human being." I paused and glanced at the still unopened door I had been knocking on. "Um, do you know, is this Gavin's room or is it the one on the other side? I forgot which one he said it was."

"No, you had the right room," Kevin said.

"Oh, I was just coming by to thank him for checking in on me yesterday," I said, speaking probably entirely too fast. I was overexplaining. I needed to peel back, but I felt like I couldn't stuff the words back in my mouth fast enough. "He was just really nice to do that, and I wanted to check in with him."

"Well, that's too bad," Kevin said. "You missed him. He took off."

"What?"

"Yeah, he left an hour or two ago. Didn't even say goodbye or anything. Someone said he might have gone home, but I don't know if they actually talked to him."

"Oh, anyone know why?"

Kevin shrugged.

"Maybe he caught a bug or something," he said, then his face dropped a little as he noticed my shoulders slump. "I mean, he could have caught it from anywhere, Lila. I'm not insinuating he got something from you. It's just it's not like him to bail like that."

"I see," I said.

"He usually texts me if he's going to go somewhere," Kevin continued. "If he was just going out for a burger or something, I think I'd know. I tried texting him twice, but he hasn't answered. But, I mean, it's only been an hour or two. He could just be out doing something. I don't know if I believe all that about him going home."

"I just hope I didn't get him sick," I said, my voice sounding far away. My mind was racing, but I had to keep from letting on the true thoughts in my head. Not in front of Kevin.

"Well, I wouldn't stress about it," he said. "Gavin's a big boy. If he came over and got sick, then that's on him, not you." He stepped out of his room a bit more, keeping his foot in the door so it didn't close behind him. "Don't worry about it. I'm sure he'll turn up sooner or later. Do you want me to let you know if he texts me?"

"Oh, no, that's okay," I said, trying to fake the cheery smile of someone that isn't wildly concerned and desperately wants to know immediately if he messages him back. "I'm sure I'll see him when he gets back at some point. If you could just tell him I came by to thank him for checking in on me. I'm doing that with everyone that came by or brought me something."

"Sure," Kevin said. "I'd have brought you something if I had known."

He looked sad, and I had the impulse to hug him. Kevin, despite being such a big man, was extremely sensitive and sweet. It was a shame he didn't have someone, but at the same time, he seemed awfully content on his own.

"I appreciate that," I said. "I was overwhelmed with everything people brought me. I'm good. Just let Gavin know I came by if you see him, if you could."

"Of course," he said. "Good night, Lila."

"Good night, Kevin."

Smiling, he closed the door, slipping back inside to what sounded like soft music and the hint of something spicy and warm. There was a curry place down the street from the hotel, and I got the faintest whiff of a smell that reminded me of it. *Lucky Kevin*, I thought. *I could go for a good curry.*

As I walked to the elevator, though, my thoughts went back to Gavin. If he'd left that suddenly, he probably had a reason. And it probably was me. One way or the other, I was likely the reason he'd left.

I felt horrible about it.

What if I had gotten him sick? This tournament was so important to him, he had talked about it a lot over the last few weeks. He was going to be seen by a few other scouts during it, and it was the culmination of a lot of hard work over the winter to get ready for it. If I got him sick by having him cuddle with me in the bed and breathing my germs onto him, I would feel terrible about the opportunity that I'd ruined.

Kevin had said not to worry, that if Gavin got sick, it was his own fault, but how could I really believe that? Gavin didn't have to spend that much time with me, but he felt obligated to as my friend. I really should have been more forceful about making him leave so he could get rest and prepare for the games.

Of course, there was the other possibility too. A worse one. That somehow, he was so embarrassed about what he did, about how we were so familiar with each other as we hung out, that he just left. That either he chose to not stay at the hotel or he simply went home. Somewhere far away from me.

It felt like a dark cloud was hanging over my head by the time I got back to my room and opened the door. Before I could even close it behind me, tears were stinging the corners of my eyes. How could I be so stupid? How could I even let myself fantasize about him, when just hanging out with me while I was sick made him run away in embarrassment? Or shame.

Or both.

My eyes fell on the bag of games that he had brought over, including the plastic cup with the dice in it. Angrily, I picked them up, shoving them all into a small ball in the bag and then tossing them in a drawer. I didn't want to look at them. I didn't want to think about him. I needed to get him out of my mind, get some rest, and go play softball tomorrow. Like I was here to do.

And I needed to leave Gavin alone.

# Chapter Seven

## *Gavin*

I GLANCED AT MY WATCH and sighed.

It was almost eight.

Where the hell was she?

The little coffee shop was only a few blocks from the hotel, close enough that I could actually see it in the distance from the corner booth by the window I was sitting in. I took a sip of the coffee and checked my phone again.

Eight on the dot.

She'd said she would be here at seven-thirty, and yet, Mom was nowhere to be found. I had texted. I had sent messages to her almost entirely *Minion* themed social media. I had even called. Nothing. It wasn't like it was unlike her to be unreliable about being somewhere she was supposed to be—memories of baseball games I had to get rides home with from Kevin's parents would attest to that—but this seemed weird even for her. Where would she go? She didn't know Myrtle Beach well enough to just go off, right?

*Five more minutes*, I told myself. *Five more minutes and then I'm out of here. There's no reason to stick around if she isn't coming.* If she decided to go drink or whatever it was she was doing and completely skipped out on seeing me after somehow finding my room and leaving a note, then I was going to just not bother with her at all.

A shift in my peripheral vision caught my attention. The coffee shop was surprisingly busy for this time of evening, but one person stood out among the crowd. Unlike the mostly early-twenty-somethings standing around and drinking lattes and other drinks that barely qualified as coffee, he was sipping a single cup out of one of those little porcelain mugs they only gave to black coffee drinkers.

He had also been there since before I got there. And had been occasionally looking over at me.

At first, I thought maybe he was a coach from another one of the teams. It wasn't unusual for opposing teams to get in a day early and hang out in the city, nor was it that weird that a coach from another team would recognize me. I was kind of a big deal. But this guy didn't look like a baseball coach. He was short, for one thing, but wide. He was built like a very muscular bowling ball. He was also wearing a leather jacket, inside, in the heat.

I glanced over at him and saw beads of sweat on his bald head being wiped off with a napkin as his eyes darted away. From me.

He was trying not to be noticed. The problem was, I had noticed him. In fact, I thought I might even recognize him now that I got a good look at him. If I was right, then something was most certainly off.

I hit the button to call my mother again, and as it rang four times, I was about to leave a message when there was a click.

"Hello?" Mom said on the other end.

"Mom?" I asked. "Where the hell are you?"

"That's no way to speak to your mother, Gavin," she said, always aware of an opportunity to establish some power structure in a conversation.

"You said you'd be at the coffee shop at seven-thirty. It's after eight. Where are you?"

"Oh, sorry, son," she said, almost flippantly. "I had to go home."

"What? I tried calling and messaging you. Didn't you think you should tell me?"

"I was *driving*," she said, emphasizing the word to appeal to the idea of the danger of messaging or talking while driving. It was bullshit, since I had personally witnessed her text and make calls while driving. Hell, I had watched her compete in online Texas Hold 'Em games on her phone while driving. "I had to wait until I got home to call you."

"But you didn't call me. I called you," I said.

She made a disgusted sound, the kind she always made when I caught her in some inconvenient bit of non-truth telling.

"Gavin, it was an emergency. I wasn't thinking straight."

"What emergency?"

"Your father," she said. She almost didn't have to say anything else. It was always Dad. "He's in some deep shit, Gavin. As a matter of fact, you need to keep your eyes peeled yourself."

"Why?" I asked. "Why would I need to keep *my* eyes peeled? What has he done this time? And why would you come all the way out here to tell me personally rather than call me, and then leave before you could meet me?"

"I had to," she said. "Look, I'm not going home. I'm going somewhere else." She sighed. "I was trying not to distract you, but I am heading south down the border of South Carolina right now. I am on the run."

"From what?"

"I just—I thought I escaped them. I thought heading to the ocean would lose them, and when I realized I was heading toward Myrtle Beach, I figured I could come see you and tell you what was going on. I didn't think they would follow me. I'm sorry. But when I got there and found where your room was, I left a note and then saw them watching me. I had to leave. I think I lost them in Myrtle Beach, but I'm worried they know you are there now."

"Mom, what is going on?"

"I told you. It's your father. He's in some deep shit this time."

"He's always in deep shit," I said. "That's what he does."

"Gavin, stop it!" she shouted. She took a moment, seemingly breathing heavily, her voice faltering when she spoke. Like she was holding back tears. "This is different."

I put my head in my hand and pushed the coffee away from me. The last thing I needed was more to make my nerves on edge.

The problem was, I didn't know how much of this to believe. Neither of them were heavily into drugs, mostly preferring to drink their lives away, but it wasn't like they didn't occasionally do drugs too. As a matter of fact, this wasn't the first time my mother had called me on the run from something she believed to be following her because Dad had done something terrible.

The difference was, when it happened before, I was at home, Mom was in Montana of all places, and Dad was at the shop. They had done LSD, and Mom had a bad trip, convinced herself that demons and angels were at war in the shop and that Dad had killed one of them with a tire iron. She got in a car and drove until she ended up in Montana two days later, unsure of how she got there or what was going on. I only knew why she left because Dad had wandered home later, coming down from the trip, and told me the story.

As for the angel he had supposedly killed, it was a cardboard stand-up advertisement of Shaquille O'Neil hawking some weird motorcycle motor oil.

But this sounded different. For one, Mom didn't sound as frantic or unintelligible as she had when she called me from Montana, or from the voicemails Dad had played for me when he was trying to find her. She sounded sober, even. And terrified.

"Okay," I said, trying to keep my composure. "What happened? Explain it to me."

Out of the corner of my eye, the man in the leather jacket stood. He took his mug to the counter and set it among the other dirty dishes that were there and turned his back to me. Briefly, he seemed to look back at me as he pushed through the door leading outside, and I thought we made eye contact. Then he was outside in the increasing darkness. Out of sight.

"I can't," she said. "I'm so scared, Gavin."

"Mom, you were fine like two minutes ago. Have you been drinking? Taking drugs?"

"Gavin, I am terrified. I was trying not to worry you," she said. "But the more I think about it, the more I think you might be in danger too. These men are not to be messed with."

"Who?" I asked. "Who aren't to be messed with?"

"The biker gang," she said. "The snakes, or eight-balls, or whatever they are called."

"Eights and Aces?" I asked.

"Yes, that," she said. "Those men. They... they are very angry at your father. And me. And I am afraid they might take it out on you."

"How?" I said. "And why? I have nothing to do with anything."

"They don't care, Gavin," she said. "These are ruthless men. Awful men. Your father is a fucking idiot for getting involved with them. But he kept telling me, no, they are fine. They just want his help. But they didn't, Gavin. They wanted his life. He's screwed us over. All of us."

"Mom, slow down. What happened?" I asked.

"Your father. He was... he was helping hide money for them. In the shop."

"Oh shit," I said.

I could see where this was going. Dad could not be trusted with cash. Not even my piggy banks were safe as a kid. He would routinely take little bits from what tiny amount I had to pay for essential things like gas or food, all because he'd blown his money at the bar or gambling. It was always on me to help supplement my own dinner through buying groceries out of my savings.

I could only imagine what stupidity he'd gotten into if someone was dumb enough to leave money in his presence for more than ten minutes.

"He's an idiot, your father," she said. "I love him, but he's stupid, Gavin. Stupid, stupid, stupid."

"What did he do?"

"He spent it," she said plainly. "All of it. He spent all of it. He kept saying he could make it back, but then there was less and less of it. And he kept finding things he needed to pay for. Then they came back asking about it, and he didn't have it. He told them he had to go get it, that he moved it out of the shop for safekeeping."

"Then what?"

"Then he found me at the hair salon, gave me an envelope with two hundred dollars in it and said to run. Immediately," she said. "He said not to use our cards, not that they had anything on them. He said to just run. To put as much in the tank as possible and go. That he would call me when he could."

"When was that?"

"Three days ago," she said. "Gavin, I am so worried."

"Mom, if something happened to him, they wouldn't be looking for you," I said. "They would have already done what they wanted to Dad."

"No, Gavin," she said, her voice dropping low and serious. "Not these men. They will hurt everyone he knows until they get their money. Gavin, they will come after you if you aren't careful."

I sighed.

"Mom, how much money does Dad owe these people?"

My voice was monotone. In the back of my mind, I wondered if this was just some elaborate plan to get my scholarship money. If it was, she was going all the way for it. But if I could give them a couple thousand dollars and shut them up long enough to get through the season, as much as I hated it, maybe it was worth it. Especially when the other option was dealing with situations like this.

"Twenty grand," she said.

There was silence for a moment as I swallowed the enormity of what she'd told me. I didn't have twenty grand to just give away. Hell, that was pretty much every dime I had in savings, and I would still need to survive.

"Twenty thousand dollars?" I confirmed.

"Yes," she said, her voice trembling like she was on the edge of tears. Real ones. Not the ones she often employed when she felt like she was trying to get something she wanted. But the ones that really sounded like she was being completely honest with her terror.

"Mom, that's a lot of money. How did he spend all that?"

"I told you," she said. "He's an idiot. He bought things. Stupid things. So many stupid things."

"And you kept asking me for money?" I asked.

"Gavin, I was trying to pay it back!" She was sobbing on the other end now. I would feel bad for her if I didn't also feel the incredible weight of making this right for them. Of fixing it for them. Of cleaning up their mess. Again. "I just wanted to fix it."

On the other side of the window, looking out toward the street that led to the hotel, I could see the man in the leather jacket again. His bald head shone in the light from the streetlight above him. He was waiting.

For me. I knew it in my bones. He was waiting for me.

What the hell was I going to do?

"Mom, I have to go," I said. "Call me when you feel like you are in a safe place."

"All right," she said. "Gavin, please take care of yourself."

"I will," I said.

I watched as the bald man lit up a cigarette and turned away from the shop.

What was I going to do?

# Chapter Eight

## *Lila*

I FELT LIKE SHIT.

Not just because of the sickness that had been plaguing me the last couple of days, but now I had the weight of whatever was going on with Gavin hanging over me too. And as much as I wanted to not think about it and take Kevin's advice, I couldn't stop. The idea that I had either made him sick or worse, it made him sick to his stomach about what happened last night, kept rolling over my thoughts, steamrolling over them, in fact. I couldn't think about anything for more than five minutes without a sense of guilt dropping down on my head all over again.

With all the games shoved in a drawer, all the other girls having a quiet night in after the wild night the night before, and also kind of avoiding me because I had been sick, there wasn't much to do. I was stuck in a hotel room twiddling my fingers at eight in the evening.

Maybe I could sleep early. If I tried, I could probably get myself to sleep around nine if I lay down now. It would be difficult, sure, but if I took another one of my cold medicine pills, maybe I could convince myself to hit the sack.

Deciding to hold off on the over-the-counter anti-cold medicine until later if I really couldn't sleep, I slid inside my bed and turned the television on. Thankfully, the hotel had one of the cooking channels, and I put it on with the volume low and lay back, trying to will myself to relax.

But the more I tried to relax, the more memories of the night before would flash through my mind. And then the guilt would come right after it. It was a losing effort. I knew it was a losing effort. And yet, I kept trying anyway.

Suddenly, my phone pinged with the notification sound for a text message. I reached over to the nightstand and pulled it toward me as it pinged again. And again. And again.

It was Star, speaking in her trademarked barrage of single-line thoughts. She typed like she spoke, one sentence at a time, always teetering on the edge of her thoughts going somewhere else and shooting off into a different tangent. It was like speaking with a drunken puppy. She was adorable, but hard to understand and easily distracted.

She was running down her day the day before, giving me a play-by-play of everything she'd done, starting with waking up to a breakfast of mostly cheese and bread and going to bed with wine, more bread, and more cheese. Secretly I kind of hoped it caught up with her and she would return to Georgia several pounds heavier, but I knew better. Star could eat an entire horse and somehow lose weight. She had a magical unicorn gift, and I resented it.

The pinging sound was constant, only spaced out by how long it took her to type them. I realized she was just ending her day in France, and even if she did recognize the time difference, likely assumed I was still going this early in the evening anyway. For her, it was two in the morning. She was crawling into bed half-drunk and excited to brag. I was somehow even sadder than just being in the States and not living her life by trying to get into bed and asleep before there were even two digits in the PM side of the clock.

I watched the messages come in, not clicking on them but seeing what the preview would allow me to see until I just couldn't take it anymore. She was enjoying her time there, that was for sure. She kept mentioning people's names, ones I didn't recognize. Either they were friends of hers whose names I'd never bothered to commit to memory, which admittedly was most of them, or they were new friends she'd met in France. Several of the names could be boys or girls. Again, I felt a hint of protectiveness for Gavin that was wholly inappropriate.

Tapping the silent button, the pinging sound stopped, and I sighed as I set the phone down. I would wait a little while, until she was done and asleep before I would read her texts. Then maybe I would respond. In a few hours. When it would be the middle of the night for her.

That was probably mean of me. Part of me insisted it was just so she would wake up to a message from me, but another part, a darker part, knew full well that I would enjoy the thought of waking her from her perfect, stressless, half-drunken slumber. Even knowing she would probably just smile and put the phone back down, going back to sleep without a worry in her mostly empty mind, the fact that it would disrupt any sweet dreams gave me the tiniest bit of glee.

"I am an awful person," I sighed at myself.

Sleeping wasn't happening. Not yet, anyway. I was still a good half hour away from my self-imposed deadline of taking any more medicine that could help me sleep, so I slipped out of the bed and made my way to the window overlooking the beach, and less sexily, the parking lot.

The heavy curtains had been drawn since the daytime, but I opened them now, letting the last of the dying sunlight fill the room, along with the creeping darkness that made the sky a swirl of red and orange and purple and blue, like one of those cocktails they sold at clubs Star had dragged me to. Not often, mind. But once or twice.

I looked out over the beach and temporarily thought about going out and walking on it, letting the water wash over my feet and listening to the waves crash. It might be nice. Granted, the music was already blaring out of the clubs nearby, and there were lots of people down there too. It wouldn't be as peaceful as I was probably thinking, but if

I put in earbuds, maybe I could at least drown out the sound and just focus on the water.

Briefly, I wondered how silly it would be to stand at the edge of the ocean while listening to a streaming video of ocean sounds on my earbuds. I was about to go grab them and debate it on my way down to the water when I noticed something in the parking lot. Dark shapes were moving out there in the shadows created by the high wall that separated the parking lot and the beach.

A person that looked an awful lot like Gavin was down there. Or at least I thought it looked like him. It had his shape, for sure, and what colors I could make out looked like clothes I recognized him as wearing before. But there were also other shapes out there with him. Men. Large men.

They were huddled in the center of the parking lot, and the other men seemed to be surrounding the Gavin-figure. It looked highly intimidating. There was clearly an animated conversation happening. My window was capable of opening slightly, not enough to slip outside of, but enough to let the sounds of the ocean and the cool air in when that was applicable. Our school might have paid for hotel rooms for us, but they weren't about to pay for rooms with luxuries like balconies.

At least, not for me.

I was tempted to roll the window open with the old-school tool that looked like a window opener from an old car when the men seemed to back off and disperse. I wasn't sure what I would have yelled out of the window, especially since I didn't actually know if it was Gavin, but part of me wanted to shout down there and break up whatever was going on anyway. It looked... weird.

But as the men backed up and disappeared past where I could see them, out toward the strip, I let go of the handle that I realized I was already gripping. The man who looked like Gavin seemed to watch them go, putting his hands on his hips for a moment, then one hand going up to the back of his neck. Then he turned smartly and began to head into the side-door of the hotel.

Maybe I should go check Gavin's room one more time? If I gave him ten minutes or so, maybe I could drop by and just see if he was there. If that was Gavin down there, I was curious to know what had happened. They certainly hadn't looked friendly.

I reached for the phone again and noticed that there were over a dozen other messages from Star. She had kept peppering my phone with more inane chatter about whatever it was Star thought was important enough to tell me about, and I again felt a little guilt about how jealous I was of her. She thought enough of me as a friend to message me when she was on this great vacation. I was being a jerk. I should probably read her messages and respond now.

But there was another message waiting for me. One that wasn't from Star. It had been sent in just the last few seconds.

From Gavin.

I clicked it open eagerly, sitting down hard on the bed.

"Feeling any better?" the message said.

"I am," I typed back. "Lots better. I took the day off of practice, but I'll be good to go tomorrow, for sure."

"Cool," he typed back. "Good to hear." There was a beat between messages, long enough for me to wonder if that was all there was going to be, and then another came in. "Have you eaten dinner yet?"

I stared at the message for a moment, unsure of what to do. Technically, yes, I had eaten dinner. If dinner was cereal and was eaten at four in the afternoon. I frankly hadn't had much of an appetite, especially after I went to visit Gavin and he hadn't been there. I might have munched through some crackers, but it would have been mindlessly. I saw empty wrappers in the room, but I was mystified as to when I'd eaten them. For all I knew, Gavin had eaten them the night before.

"No," I typed, untyped, retyped, and then went through that cycle about six times before I finally sent.

"Are you hungry?" he typed back almost instantly.

"Starving," I said, realizing as I hit the send button that I was. It had come out of nowhere, but yes, I was in fact really hungry.

"Well, I am down at the bar downstairs," he typed back, then the little bubbles that delineated his typing seemed to go on forever before the next message came in. "Want to join me?"

"I'll be down in a few minutes," I typed back.

As I put the phone down on the bed, I fought the urge to squeal.

Not only was he not at home, sick because of me, but he wasn't seemingly upset with me either. He had, in fact, asked me to join him for dinner. A dinner that I was fairly sure was going to be sans-other members of the teams. I had been on their floor and knew most of them were already in their rooms, nursing hangovers and getting rest before tomorrow.

A dinner. With just us. At a hotel.

I took a deep breath. I needed to let all these nerves go. This was just a meal with a friend; the location was purely coincidental. He was still Star's boyfriend, despite all the boys she was apparently meeting in France and hanging out with until all hours of the night. I presumed. He was my friend. My friend who had been worried about me and helped nurse me back to health.

I owed him a dinner to thank him.

Armed with an approach that was entirely detached from reality, I convinced myself that I was joining him not because I was fighting a crush that was becomingly wildly problematic, but because I owed him some company after he helped me out. That I was doing *him* a favor.

And if I was going to do him such a favor, the least I could do was look presentable.

Tearing my clothes off, I grabbed my makeup bag and started applying eyeliner and powder and lipstick faster than I ever had in my life. Then, when I had a face that looked marginally better than the one I had without the aid of Revlon, I pulled open the drawer that had only one thing in it and pulled it out. The sundress was going to have to do.

I slipped it on over top of a pair of leggings that I loved because they had three pockets, slipped the key card in my back pocket, and grabbed my phone, shoving it down in the tiny pocket on my hip.

As I shut the door behind me quietly, I could barely wipe the smile off my face.

# Chapter Nine

## *Gavin*

I WAS FRAZZLED AS HELL, and when I sat down at the booth in the little restaurant/bar area of the hotel, I was still shaking. I needed to talk to someone, even if it wasn't about what had just gone on. I just needed to talk. To try to reset my brain into being normal. Anything other than the creeping anger and fear that had filled my body since I'd walked out of the coffee shop and proceeded to be followed all the way back to the hotel.

At first it had just been the one guy. I thought I might be able to take him. Then he was joined by another. And another. When I got into the parking lot of the hotel, my only solace was that it was still technically daylight, and a bunch of windows faced the parking lot. Surely, they wouldn't try to do something when they were so visible. Right?

One look at their eyes when I heard my name and turned toward them told me that was untrue. These were men who didn't mind being seen. Because they would keep their cool in a situation that other people wouldn't. Because they had done it many times before.

My fingers were still jittering on the table when Lila's last text came in. She was on her way down.

I didn't even know what I was doing asking her to dinner. It was probably the wrong kind of message to send, but I had typed it before thinking. I needed someone other than Kevin to talk to. Kevin wasn't the guy to let know that anyone was threatening me, ever, unless I wanted to start a war.

As the catcher, he was fiercely protective of his pitchers, and as my long-time friend, it was doubly so for me. If I had told him about what happened out there, he likely would have changed into boots, put on gloves, and told me it was time to go find those guys and put a hurt on them. They would have killed him before he had a chance, but he would try. No way any of them would want to get into a fistfight with a man that looked like a mountain. They would just shoot him.

The problem with all that was Kevin would have no idea what he was getting into. I had spent our entire lives trying to keep my parents—and the kind of life they lived—away from everyone. Kevin knew they weren't great parents, and his folks seemed to know about them in a passing sort of way that normal people knew about drug addicts and drunks. But they didn't know about Dad and his constant desire to get involved in money-making schemes. About his flirtation with biker gangs and mobs.

About how, as Mom put it, absolutely stupid he was.

Not that I thought it would make Kevin think any differently of me, not now, anyway. Not as adults. But he wouldn't take it seriously enough. He would think he could handle it.

A waiter came by the table, clearly non-plussed at having someone sit in the booths at this time of evening rather than hang out at the bar, and I ordered a beer. The eye roll that followed before he asked for my ID was enough to temporarily make me not think about the terror of the few minutes before and instead want to toss him through a window. After I gave him my ID and he handed it back, I told him I had someone joining me, and the visible slump of his shoulders was enough that if I were a petty man would have eliminated any chance of a tip.

As the waiter walked away, Lila appeared at the elevator, coming out of it and looking toward the bar area with a smile. I felt my chest tighten as she walked toward me, and I stood. The pull toward her was strong, so strong that I didn't even process what I was doing until my arms were wrapped around her in a tight hug that lingered far too long.

But, as I noticed, she wasn't trying to break the embrace either.

"Good to see you looking better," I said, trying to sound casual.

"Yeah, I feel great," she said. I wasn't sure if she was just saying that or not, but regardless, she *looked* great.

Her hair was pulled back in a ponytail like she often had it while playing or studying, but she was wearing a breezy dress that showed off more of her chest than I was used to seeing. It was clearly the kind of thing that someone wears to the beach, maybe over a bikini, though it was appropriate for what we were doing too.

Which was dinner. Just dinner. I had to repeat that to myself. Just dinner.

We sat down, and the waiter returned with my beer and then eyed Lila suspiciously.

"May I see your ID?" he asked.

"Oh, I'm not drinking," she said. "I am over twenty-one, but I'll just have a water, thanks."

"Of course," he said, and I wondered if it was dripping with sarcasm or disappointment that the bill wouldn't be higher.

"Don't want a cocktail or anything? My treat," I said.

"No, no, thank you," she said. "Need to rehydrate. Besides, this is my treat, not yours."

"I don't think so," I began, but she had already pulled a menu up and shushed me.

"You came and took care of me while I was sick. Least I can do is buy you a meal. Now do you know if the burgers are any good?"

I smiled.

"I heard they're great. Kevin said so anyway," I said.

"Kevin seems to know his food," she said. "When I met him, he was so much of a frat boy, but have you noticed how he's turning into a grown up all of a sudden?"

"I have noticed that," I said. "His wine evenings are my favorite new wrinkle of his."

"I actually smelled something like curry coming from his room earlier," she said. "Smelled delicious."

"Wait, you went up to Kev's room?" I asked, cocking my head to one side.

"Oh, yeah, that," she said. "I went up to say thank you for last night. You weren't there, but Kevin was. He stuck his head out and talked to me for a minute."

"Ahh," I said.

"Hey, are you okay?" she asked.

I froze.

"What?"

"It's just that your hands… you're tapping on the table."

"Oh," I said, looking down at my fingers, which indeed were doing a Billy Joel impression on the table. I shoved them down in my lap and tried to put on a smile. "Yeah, I'm just amped up over some stuff."

I wanted to tell her. I wanted to tell her about my parents. About how they had done this all my life, and now it was just escalating. Just when I thought that, as an official adult, I wouldn't have to deal with their bullshit anymore, it was just getting worse. That the men tonight had really freaked me out, and the things they said… I wasn't going to be able to forget them any time soon.

"Look, you don't have to say anything. I understand," she said.

"What?" I asked, confused yet again. I felt like I was stumbling backwards in this conversation, unable to get a strong foothold with everything else racing through my mind. Not the least of which was how soft her skin looked, and my desperate attempt to not look directly into the center of her chest. How that clearly defined Y-shape where her breasts met seemed so… lickable.

"I get it," she said. "I really do. Last night was a mistake."

My stomach dropped, and it felt like a hot rock had been slipped down inside.

"A mistake?" I repeated.

"Yeah," she said, her voice rising a pitch like she was trying to convince me but wasn't entirely all that sure herself. "A mistake. I should have just let you go back to your room earlier. It was really stupidly selfish of me to want your company like that, and I don't want you to feel weird about it at all. You were just helping a sick friend not feel so pitiful." She was smiling, but there was something else behind her expression.

"Yeah," I muttered.

"Star will understand," she said. There it was. That was what this was all about. Star.

My girlfriend.

"Right," I said.

"I mean, she knows we are friends," she continued, her eyes locked firmly on the menu. "We've been friends since you started tutoring me. No big deal. And you know how she is, all hippie-like. She will understand us falling asleep was just two friends zoning out. No different than all three of us doing that on the couch back at home. That's what I'm going to tell her when I call her later. But really, she won't mind, I don't think. And if she does, I'll let her know it's on me. I was the one who kept you up late just to take care of my pitiful, sick ass."

I was confused. And kind of angry.

"Wait, have you spoken to Star?"

She looked up from the menu for just a second, catching my eyes and then looking back at it as she flipped it over to the dessert side.

"Sort of," she said. "She's sent me a few messages. I sent a few back earlier, but you know how it is. Time zones."

"Right," I said.

Time zones. I wasn't entirely sure where she was, but wherever it was, she'd had all day to contact me and hadn't. She hadn't contacted me in a long while. Her supposed boyfriend.

"Where is she?" I asked.

"France," Lila said. "Some chateau her friend got them through some family member, I think. I honestly kind of tuned out the story, but you know how Star is. Life just kind of hands her these awesome things, and she just goes along with it and doesn't really appreciate it." She paused for a moment and then looked sheepish. "That was mean. I shouldn't talk about my best friend like that."

"It's fine if it's true," I said.

She shrugged.

"Anyway, she's lying around on a beach mostly, hanging out with some friends."

Something in the way she said that felt like there was more to the story than she was saying. Like perhaps there was more to the friends she was hanging out with that bothered Lila. I knew it had to be at least a little difficult that Lila viewed Star as her best friend when it was very clear that Star was incapable of having a best friend for herself. Whichever friend she was around at that moment was her best friend. Whoever interested her the most at that moment was her best friend.

And currently, that was probably someone on a beach in France.

It certainly wasn't Lila. Or me, for that matter.

"Who did she go there with, do you know?" I asked, trying to pry a bit. I felt like I was entitled to at least a little bit of information considering we were technically dating.

"Amber?" she said. "I don't really know. Like I said, I kind of checked out when she went on about the details. You should just call her. But when you do, just wait until I've had a chance to talk to her about last night before you do. I think it would be better coming from me so you don't have to feel awkward about it."

"Okay," I said, unconvinced.

"Seriously, just let me do it. It will be better that way. There's nothing for us to feel ashamed about. It's okay. We're just friends. We were just hanging out. But it can be weird to talk about when one person is so far away, and I know how to talk to her. It'll be better if I do it."

She was smiling still, but I could see that whatever it was behind the smile was eating at her.

I swallowed it all as the waiter came back. The bikers, the threats, Star, France, the way Lila's body looked incredible inside the dress, all of it. I shoved it down as far as I could. Nodding, I looked down at the menu and chose something at random as the waiter began talking. I didn't hear a word of it, but I didn't think I needed to. He was mostly talking to Lila, anyway.

To her chest, anyway.

"I'll have the rodeo burger," I said when his eyes reluctantly floated back over to me. "And another beer. Keep them coming, actually."

"Yes, sir," he said, straightening up and rolling his eyes again. If he did it one more time, I might just put him through a window.

I looked back at Lila, who grinned as she sipped her water through a straw. And I couldn't fight the thought going through my mind that I had never been jealous of a straw before.

# Chapter Ten

## *Lila*

I FELT FANTASTIC WHEN I woke up. Better than I had felt in a while, actually, and it got me to wondering if maybe I was beginning to feel sick before I even left. At any rate, I was up and energetic not long after the sun rose, and went down to get my breakfast well before anyone else. I was already done and heading back upstairs when most of my teammates started dragging themselves to the lobby to grab whatever they could eat and drink quickly.

Heading back to my room, I showered quickly and got dressed. It was the last full day of practice before the games started, and I wanted to get some extra batting practice in. If I headed down early, I could beat most of the team down and probably impress Coach enough that I wouldn't suffer the dreaded drop in the lineup that he was so famous for doing with any player that missed a practice.

As it was, I was used to hitting second in the order when I wasn't pitching. Even when I was pitching, he often had me hit early in the lineup, but he preferred to keep me in the traditional nine-hole. I was looking forward to a day of working out hard and seeing what I had in me after the sickness had finally gone away. I didn't have a whole lot of time to get back into fighting shape before the games, and if I needed to drive myself into the dirt today to get ready for it, I was prepared to do so.

A weight had been lifted off my shoulders in a way last night. Gavin had seemed almost disappointed when I had described how I should have sent him away. And I couldn't help but notice his eyes float down once or twice to my low-cut dress. It made me feel pretty good about myself, even if I chastised myself for letting that thought creep back in the forefront of my mind.

No, now it was time to focus on what I was here for. Competition. Winning. Glory.

And keeping my scholarship.

I headed down to the field and found myself alone for a good ten minutes before our hitting coach and two other girls joined me. I had been doing a soft toss against the cage behind the batter's box, letting my arm warm up when they came in, and silently they joined me, turning it into a triangle toss. A few minutes later, the coach walked out to the mound with a bucket of softballs, and again silently, we looked at each other, deemed me the first to go, and they took their places in short left and short right field.

I went back to the bench, opened up my bat bag, and grabbed my favorite bat. Taking a few experimental swings, I stretched with it over my head, bent at the waist, and then went into the batter's box with an eye on crushing the first pitch I saw.

Without a catcher there, until the next girl arrived, Coach was going to be lobbing easy pitches at me, not wanting to loiter behind the plate and give the other girls some practice running down fly balls. Too bad I had no intention of letting them catch anything.

The first pitch was a floating sinker, almost shoulder height. I let my weight hang back on my back foot as long as possible, and as I swung through, I didn't even feel the bat hit the ball. The usual shock of aluminum bats and heavy softballs would send a reverberation up my shoulder, but this was smooth as silk. The ball shot off the bat like a cannon, and I admired it as it took off for center field.

As it sailed over the fence, Coach turned back to me and nodded. He grabbed another ball and tossed again, and again, I launched it out of the park. The other two girls didn't even move when the bat made contact. They knew.

"All right, Barry Bonds," Coach said jokingly. "See if you can crank this one."

He wound up, surprisingly good form for a man who had never played professional softball, and fired one in low and in. Technically, it was a fastball. But Coach was in his forties and was used to tossing overhand as a baseball player all his career. His spin rate on an underhand pitch left a lot to be desired.

I crushed it, high and deep over the fence in left field, pulling it just enough to give it the angle, but not enough to go foul. It sailed far out of our view, and as it disappeared out of sight, Coach whistled.

"I hope to shit that doesn't hit someone's car," he said. "Sheesh, Lila, we give you one day off, and you come in like Sammy Sosa."

"Yeah, well," I said, "I don't like being sick. I'm making up for lost time."

"Save some of it for the game, will you?" he laughed. "Why don't you and Sanchez switch until we have a catcher and someone to go fetch your home run balls?"

I laughed and nodded, heading back to the bench to change out of batting gloves and into my fielder's glove.

The rest of batting practice came about an hour later when we had almost the full team down. I went back to smashing balls deep, though not all of them ended up out of the park. A few dinged off the fence, and one or two ended up popped up at the plate. All things considered, I was very happy with how it turned out.

Then it was time for me to switch up and go with the pitching coach. As I made my way to the bullpen, I saw that there was only one other girl there pitching. I looked at Coach Franklin and motioned to Rea, the girl working out.

"She's starting the first game?"

"No," Coach said. "You are."

"Me?" I asked. "After I missed practice?"

"Trust me, I was as surprised as you were," he said. "But Coach said you've got the ball. She's on tap as the first reliever and is working out for long relief in case we need to pull you early."

"You won't have to," I said.

"If your pitching is anything like your hitting today, I would think not."

I took the mound in the bullpen beside Rea and nodded. She smiled meekly. Rea was young, a sophomore who showed lots of promise. Thus far, she had only been used in late relief, but if they were working her arm out, they thought there was a possibility she could be a starter. I could feel intimidated by that, but I didn't. Today, I just felt too good.

The first pitch I threw was like cutting through butter with a hot knife. It was intensely satisfying. My arm was already warm from tossing and taking BP, and I fired the first pitch in near my high-water mark speed. The next few pitches inched up closer to it. Then I started working on my breaking pitches.

Everything was working. I felt like I was not working out whatever stress and frustration I had with the whole Gavin and Star situation by channeling all of it into focus on the ball. I felt like my fingers could feel the seams better, and the ball did what I wanted it to more. I was just playing better, all the way around.

As practice ended, I packed up my bag and tossed it over my shoulder, heading out of the field and back toward the hotel, past the field where the boys were doing their practice. Some of the girls were huddled behind the cage behind home plate, and I joined them without them noticing.

Gavin was on the mound, watching something going on in the out-field before the catcher caught his attention. Then he stomped his spot on the mound, rocked back, and fired a sizzling strike.

Watching his motion was like watching poetry. It was so clean, so fluid it almost made you forget that throwing a ball overhand at that speed wasn't a totally natural movement of the body. Like a world-class dancer executing a pirouette, his body just moved the way that he want-ed it to, and with a grace and power that seemed other-worldly, the ball left his hand at just the right split second and went right into Kevin's catcher's mitt.

The radar gun lit up. Ninety-eight miles an hour.

"Holy shit," one of the girls in front of me said. "He's going to hit a hundred one of these days."

Suddenly, Gavin looked up as he caught the ball coming back to him from Kevin, and I knew he was looking at me. He smiled and waved. I waved back before I even thought about where I was or who was around me.

Instantly, I heard whispers and giggling and saw eyes flash toward me. One girl whispered something to another, and they laughed hard. I felt embarrassment creep up my neck again, threatening to turn my skin into the shade of a tomato in the sun.

Either they thought I was hitting on him or that I was pining for something I couldn't have. Either way was pathetic. None of them would believe that he would actually be interested in me. Why should he? He was Gavin Freeman. He was a god already. I was just the curvy, too-thick jock girl who played softball.

Besides, he was dating someone. Someone *much* more appropriate.

I felt a bitterness in the back of my throat and slipped away, heading back to the hotel without another thought. If I waited a few minutes, it was likely that the boys would be done and I could actually talk to Gavin. But I didn't want to wait. What's more, I didn't want to be *seen* waiting. The last thing I needed was to look even more pathetic by being the girl who hung out, waiting for Gavin to get out of practice so he would pay attention to me.

Trying to push the negative thoughts out of my head and focus on my success on the field for the day, I made my way back inside and dropped my equipment by the head of the bed. Drawing the curtains, I decided to go ahead and disrobe in the middle of the room and toss my clothes into the laundry bag. I'd need to wash them tonight so I was ready for the game tomorrow. But first, I was going to shower.

I turned on the water and waited for it to get warm as I stood in the bathroom, cycling through music on my phone until I found something I wanted to listen to. Sticking the phone into the sink to give it a little more reverberating sound, I got into the shower and sighed as the water loosened my muscles.

My body lit up the second I touched the soap to my skin. I couldn't help it. The water was warm, and my adrenaline was still going from such a good practice. And the image of Gavin, sweat rolling down his neck as he stood on the mound, that slight grin as he waved at me, it was too much. My fingers slid down my stomach and between my thighs, parting the soft hair at my core and finding my clit.

I closed my eyes, sinking into the image. There was no stopping it anyway.

I envisioned him there with me, standing across from me in the shower. How his hands would feel on my skin. How his lips would feel on my own.

My fingers swirled over my clit while my other hand held on to the wall for support. In my mind, it was Gavin holding me up. Holding me close.

He would lift my leg, pressing my back against the wall as our lips crushed into one another. My heart would thump as I felt the head of his massive cock penetrate me. I would gasp as he filled me, and then I would tremble, begging for more. And he would deliver.

My mind raced with the fantasy of Gavin and me locked in an embrace in the shower, in the bed, on the tiny couch where he'd sat while I was sick. It raced with images of me on my back, riding him, on my knees below him. I could nearly feel the warmth of his thick, bulging cock on my tongue.

I came, sliding down the wall as I whimpered in ecstasy. Eventually, I gained control of myself again and finished my shower, deciding that, just this once, I wasn't going to feel guilty.

# Chapter Eleven

## *Gavin*

THE WEIGHT OF EVERYTHING going on with Mom and Dad was pressing down on me as I showered after practice. It had been weighing on me all practice too, distracting me as I tried to focus on the mechanics of my game. It was an off-day for pitching, but I flubbed grounders twice, and couldn't seem to make solid contact on anything breaking in batting practice.

It was enough that Coach told me I could take the rest of practice off halfway through if I was tired, but I soldiered on. Mostly because Kevin was having a banner day, and seeing his cheerful smile was at least bringing the mood up a bit.

That cheerful mood apparently didn't stop when he was out of his uniform either. I had no more than gotten on shorts after my shower when I could hear his ham-fist pounding on my door and his deep baritone singing out my name in an operatic style.

"Damn, Kev, you looking to replace Pavarotti?" I asked as I swung the door open.

"What do you know about the Three Tenors?" he laughed as he barreled past me into my room and threw himself on the tiny couch, which looked even tinier under his massive frame.

"I know you play it in the car all the time," I said. "What's going on?"

"I'll tell you what's going on," Kevin said, leaning forward so his elbows were on his knees and his eyes danced with merriment. "*We* are going to go have some fun."

"Ah, Kev, I dunno, I already—" I began.

"You did nothing of the kind, and you can't convince me of it," he said. "You weren't hanging out with me, and therefore it didn't count, boss."

I laughed and shook my head.

"I didn't get a lot of sleep last night, and we have games tomorrow," I continued to half-heartedly protest.

"All the more reason to go out tonight," he said cheerfully. "We won't have a chance after tonight, and there is alcohol to imbibe."

"Kev, no one can out-drink you, and I am pretty certain you took down an entire bottle of wine last night."

"Both of those things are true," he said. "However, they are not reasons not to go out tonight. Come on. Be my wingman."

"Wingman?" I asked. "Since when did you ever need a wingman?"

"Since I felt like convincing my buddy to go out drinking," he said.

"Fair enough," I said. "But I should get back in before last call."

"Yeah, yeah," Kevin said. "Now get dressed. Knock on my door when you're ready."

"What do you mean, get dressed? I am dressed."

He looked critically at my pair of shorts. Slowly, he shook his head.

"Nah," he said finally and walked past, exiting out of my room in a trailing mist of cologne.

Laughing, I went back to my suitcase and opened it up.

Long ago, I had watched a TV show with some well-put together dude, one whose name escaped me at the moment, but who had seemingly achieved all the things I hoped I would achieve at his age. He was well-dressed, successful, and seemed to have his shit together. The interviewer was talking to him about rising up out of poverty, and it struck me enough to make me watch it, engrossed in the man's serious but approachable attitude.

He had talked about a number of things, all of which I took to heart. One of those things that he said every successful man should have is a selection of nice dress clothes. Even if you don't expect to use them often, having them was invaluable. I put that advice to the test and found that he was wildly correct as I grew up. So much so that even now, on a baseball tournament trip to the beach, I had a nicely folded dress shirt, slacks, socks, and shoes in the suitcase, taking up space that could have gone to any number of other things but that I'd insisted on bringing.

Just in case.

As I put them on, keeping the top button undone and eschewing the tie, I checked myself in the mirror.

*I wish Lila could see this*, I thought to myself.

I mean Star. *Star.* I wish Star could see this.

Spraying on a bit of cologne, I headed for Kevin's door and rapped on it. Rather than poking his head out or simply opening the door, he swung it wide and appeared in the center, his head just missing smashing on the top of the doorframe.

"Ready?" he asked.

"As I'll ever be," I said.

"Looking good, boss," he said.

"Thanks, Kev."

"What do you think of the shoes?"

I looked down at the enormous Chucks he was wearing. Somehow it worked with the rest of the more traditional slacks and dress shirt motif.

"Blue works for you, bud," I said.

"Damn right," he said. "Come on."

It was a curious thing going out with Kevin. On one hand, he stuck out like a sore thumb, being a foot above almost everyone and looking like someone had carved him out of a tree. But there was also a specific kind of … fluidity to him. He had never addressed it with me, but perhaps he never had to. I'd known it about him since the day we met. Kevin was not a choosy person when it came to who he could have a good time with. Whoever, and however, that good time was had.

It fit with the wine and opera aspects of his personality as much as it fit with his baseball and beer kegs part. Among the many reasons I greatly enjoyed being his best friend was the fact that I never knew which Kevin I was going to get on a daily basis. Was I going to run into the heavy weight-lifting, heavy metal-listening, bearded lumberjack Kevin, or the pink shorts, clean-shaven, Bellini and philosophy conversation Kevin?

Tonight, it appeared, he was a mixture of both.

As we headed down the steps, foregoing the elevator with the ego of athletes everywhere, I figured we'd drop right off into the bar in the bottom of the hotel and start there. It was a surprise when Kevin barreled through the door and began heading for the exit, only stopping when we came across a couple of the girls coming the other way. Among them was Lila.

She looked spectacular.

It wasn't that she was wildly dressed up. She just had on jeans and a tight blouse, almost casual enough to be normal, but probably showing a bit more of her assets than strictly necessary. The jeans were an interesting touch considering the heat, but they were very shapely around her backside and showed off how long her legs were without expressly showing off how muscular they were too.

"Hey," I said.

"Hey," she responded.

"What are you up to?"

"Oh, just getting dinner," she said, motioning toward the other girls. "Coach bought us all dinner, so you know. Not going to skip that."

"For sure," I said, laughing awkwardly.

"Emma wanted to watch the sunset afterwards, so we spent some time out there. I just had no interest in getting in water."

"I see," I said, and suddenly couldn't stop my brain from imagining her in that tight, light blue blouse, soaking wet. How the shirt would cling to her breasts. How her wet hair would stick to her face and she would sling her head back to make it fall back into place behind her. How water droplets would drip down the center of her throat, racing each other as they sold their soul to be first to be between her tits.

"Gav?" Kevin said from a little ahead of me. He had turned around when he noticed I wasn't following him anymore.

"Oh, hey Kevin," Lila said. "You look nice. You both look... really nice."

"Thank you," Kevin boomed, putting on a cheesy smile and doing a half-twirl. "Look at my shoes. I got them last week."

"Chucks with slacks, I like it," Lila laughed. "You pull that off well."

"I am a man of exquisite taste, right, boss?" Kevin said, laughing.

"He is," I said.

"We're going to down to the bar a few blocks down the street. The one in here is boring and in serious need of a dance floor. The one down there has a dance floor that leads out onto the beach."

"Oh," I said. "We are?"

Kevin looked at me like I just grew a second head.

"Of course. You didn't think I wanted to hang out *here*, did you?"

"How silly of me," I said.

"I want to go!" Emma said, popping up from behind Lila. "I haven't been out dancing in weeks!"

"Me too," said Lila, and my jaw dropped. She looked at me with an expression of excitement, and I found myself warming to the idea immediately.

"Oh yeah?" I asked. "Cool, yeah, well, come on then."

"I can't go like *this!*" Emma said. "I'll be right back!"

"Sure, sure," Kevin said. "We have time. Come on, let's go grab a drink here then."

Kevin motioned toward the bar in the hotel and walked past, leaving me alone with Lila as a few other girls caught wind of the upcoming plans, squealed, and went rushing up the stairs.

"I probably should go change," Lila said, her eyes not having left mine.

"I mean, you don't have to," I said. "You look fantastic."

"Thank you," she said, then bit her bottom lip in a way that made my stomach clench. "Still, I'd feel better with a bit of eyeshadow or something. You'll wait for us?"

"I'll wait for you," I said, then realized how specifically I'd pointed that statement and clenched my jaw shut. I didn't want to backtrack it. I just let it sit there, between us, a phrase that was wholly up to interpretation and with both of us seemingly searching the other's face for which one they were going with.

"I'll be right back then," she said, and her voice seemed a bit more like a purr. My cock twitched in my slacks, and I suddenly was very happy I was wearing a slightly tighter pair of boxer-briefs.

As she walked away, I watched her go and then joined Kevin at the bar. We had no more than gotten our beers and taken a sip than Emma was back downstairs, seemingly frantic, and with more glitter on than I had ever seen one human being wear. Internally, I knew that none of us were getting out of tonight without being glitter-bombed just by being in her presence, and that meant we were going to be looking like extras from *Twilight* during the game.

Oh well, maybe we'd distract the other team with our shininess.

As Lila returned a few moments later, just ahead of the gaggle of other girls and a handful of the guys they'd picked up along the way, I sat stunned at how she looked. She had slipped into a different pair of pants, capris this time that showed off her calves and hugged the rest of her lower half like glue. She had kept the light-blue blouse but had seemingly attracted some of Emma's glitter to the cleavage. Never had I wanted to fill my face with glitter than at that moment and I chided myself for thinking it.

Her eyes were more prominent now, and they darted over to me as she grinned and I downed the beer in response.

"Hell yeah," Kevin said as he watched me finish off my beer in a few glugs. He then proceeded to take his down in what seemed an awful lot like one swallow. "Let's roll."

The group headed for the exit, and as we squeezed together to get through the door, Lila and I ended up beside each other. I could have let her go in front of me or slipped through before, but instead, I stepped halfway through and held the door with my back. She turned herself sideways and sidled past me, her chest brushing mine and her eyes drilling into my own.

I caught a whiff of her perfume as she passed me, and only for the briefest of seconds did it remind me of being in their apartment with Star. I had a feeling that was the last time I was going to think about my quasi-girlfriend all night.

I wasn't exactly mad about it.

"I didn't think you'd be the going-out type tonight," I said as we started down the sidewalk behind Kevin and the cadre of girls that was in his wake.

"Well, I was sick the first couple of days," she said. "This might be my only chance at some fun on Spring Break."

"Good point," I said. "Well, in that case, I promise to make it as fun as I can for you."

"I look forward to that," she said, giggling. The sound of her laughter made my pants tighten again, and I looked away so I wouldn't be tempted to stare at her anymore. "Oh, you know what we should do?"

"What's that?" I asked.

"We should take a selfie. For Star."

"Oh," I said. "Yeah, sure."

I pulled out my phone and held it out in front of me, turning on the camera. As I did, Lila sidled up beside me and stood on her toes in the heels she had put on. For a moment, she lost balance and caught herself on me, pressing her cheek to mine. As I snapped the picture, capturing wide, happy smiles, I found myself wanting desperately to turn her toward me and press my lips to hers. They were so close.

Lila stepped back onto her heels, and I typed out a message to Star, saying we missed her as we were heading out with the team for some dancing. I hit enter, and it sent. But as we made our way to the bar down the street, the phone never alerted that she responded. I wasn't entirely sure I would have noticed if she had.

Or cared.

# Chapter Twelve

## *Lila*

WHAT IN THE WORLD WAS I doing? I was going to get to bed early tonight.

In fact, the only reason I wasn't in pajamas right that very second was because Emma came to my door and told me Coach had bought us all food and we had to come down to the lobby to get it. I tried to talk her into bringing me my stuff, but it was no dice. She wanted me to come, and I felt like I had been a bad teammate already by being holed up in my room so long that I went.

Then when we got our food, Emma and Temika, another of the girls who seemed to never slow down at 'party time,' decided that eating outside was the best course of action so we could watch the sunset. Figuring a bit of fresh air never hurt anyone, again, I followed. And now I was wearing Emma's glitter on my boobs, which were jacked up to my chin in a tight blouse that I'd thrown on because it was the only thing I had that was remotely decent and not black, and was casually erasing the line between friendship and flirting with Gavin with a willful intent.

Not that Star seemed to care.

He sent her that picture as we walked, and I figured he would tell me if she responded. Star knew this shirt. She called it my 'only decent titty shirt.' When I pressed her on it, she stated that I should be happy to be so well endowed and not wear such 'puritanical oppres-

84

sion' clothes. Like T-shirts that didn't dip down to my belly button, I guessed.

Star was known for her eclectic sense of fashion, which may or may not involve occasional accidental nudity. I was known for wearing whatever was most comfortable depending on the weather I was in. Sweatpants and hoodies in the fall and winter, gym shorts and T-shirts in the spring and summer. Otherwise, I wore a uniform on the field or the same black dress to whatever funeral or wedding I was dragged to.

The blue blouse had been something my mother had bought me for Christmas and I'd worn exactly once to a club Star dragged me to and then put away. It showed off far more of my chest than I intended, and I was uncomfortable with the amount of attention I got, even if most of the attention was still on Star that night anyway.

I had only put it on tonight because I didn't want to wear black and seem like I was recovering from the plague. And besides, I was only going to see the girls. Right?

Now I was wearing it, prancing into a club, with the hottest guy I had ever known by my side.

*Lila, what are you doing?*

Speaking to myself in second person didn't exactly fix anything, but it made me feel better. Like I could blame someone else if something went wrong. So I kept two minds of things as we walked into the darkened club, bright yellow, blue and purple lights flashing and music thumping so loud you had to shout to be heard.

"We should stick together," Kevin bellowed, seemingly not having much trouble being heard above the din. "So we can keep an eye out. Lots of people prey on tourists."

"I don't think anyone's going to prey on you," Emma shouted, a deep grin on her face. I knew what that grin was for. That was the *I've chosen my meal for the night* grin.

Kevin shot one back at her.

"Want something to drink?"

I turned toward Gavin, who was motioning toward the bar. I nodded and followed him as he elbowed his way to a spot. Kevin followed a moment later, and the four of us were lined up together, the rest of our crew already having been lost to the darkness and the intoxicating music.

"Four shots, top shelf," Kevin said before the bartender could address Gavin.

"Whoa, hold on there, bud," Gavin said. "Don't go broke tonight."

"It's a celebration," Kevin laughed.

"Celebration of what?" Emma asked.

"Our sweeping this tourney, of course," Kevin said as the bartender poured out our shots.

"We haven't even played yet," I laughed.

"Consider this a down payment on winning," he said. "Salut!"

We clinked glasses and tipped back our drinks.

As the alcohol burned down my throat, I wondered again what I was thinking. I had really only been dragged out of my room out of guilt and a sudden and deep hunger that came from not really being able to eat for two days. Now I was downing shots in a club, knowing full well that with such little food in my stomach, I was going to be a quick drunk. No sooner had I placed the glass back down on the bar than Kevin had done a twirling motion with his finger to indicate another round.

"Woo!" Emma said as she knocked out her second shot a moment later.

"One more," Kevin said, "then we dance."

"I don't know," Gavin said.

"Hey, if you're good, you're good," Kevin said. "I won't push you. But I'm ordering you a shot, and it's up to you."

Four glasses appeared in front of us, and three of us picked them up. As I slammed the glass back on the table, my eyes met Gavin's. His fingers were loosely on the glass. I could tell he didn't really want to drink but didn't want to seem non-sociable either. Impulsively, I put my hand over his, slowly sliding my fingers between his and the glass. When it was in my grip and no longer his, I pulled it to my lips.

Our eyes never lost their connection, and I smiled devilishly as I tipped it back and swallowed. As I put the glass back down, I brushed my bottom lip with my thumb and reached out my other hand. He took it instantly.

"Dance with me?" I asked.

He didn't say a word. He didn't have to. We were already moving toward the mass of people.

We joined the rest of the crew on the floor and made a kind of circle. There wasn't much space between us, and slowly as the music switched from song to song, the space disappeared. We were right on top of each other, our bodies moving and sweat beading on the back of my neck as the alcohol kicked in. I was warm and suddenly energetic and ... *happy*.

It had been a long time since I had been this happy. A no-cares, enjoy the moment, blissful happiness. My body moved with the music instinctively, and the more we danced, the closer Gavin and I got to each other. Everyone else on the floor felt like they disappeared, becoming one gelatinous blob that I could ignore. None of them mattered. All that mattered was how Gavin's hard, athletic body moved shockingly well with the rhythm. How his hands ended up on my hips as I turned my back to him and we moved together. How my ass pressed into his crotch and I could feel the twitch of his thick cock against me.

I felt like every pore of my body was on fire. My vision was clearer than it had ever been, and yet I could barely see anything beyond Gavin's eyes. I could still taste the tequila on my tongue as I swallowed hard, trying not to say the words that were bubbling up in my chest. The words I longed to whisper in his ear. Words that formed a command that would shatter my entire reality, the tenuous place between friend and whatever it was we were moving toward. Words that would change everything.

"Kiss me."

I wanted to say it. I needed to say it. But I was fighting it, pushing it away and trying to force my brain to think rationally. I knew Star wasn't paying attention to the fact that she had a boyfriend. She didn't care. Not because she was callous or mean or intentionally cheating, but because she was incapable of thinking anything was permanent. Whatever was good in the moment was good enough.

For her, right now, Gavin didn't exist. Whatever French boy she was on the beach with did.

But I couldn't say that *for sure*, could I? She was still technically dating him. And she was my roommate, and for the lack of closer friends, my best friend. I couldn't do what I knew I wanted. What I felt like he wanted. What we could easily do right here, right now. Because it was forbidden.

And somehow, that only made it hotter.

The music was picking up tempo, getting rowdier. Kevin dragged Emma off the floor, and I could tell they were crossing every line I was desperately trying not to cross myself tonight. If he didn't end up in her room or she in his, I would be shocked. They were almost completely off the floor when Emma stopped and reached out for me, grabbing my hand and yanking me with them.

Gavin laughed and followed, wiping sweat from his brow and opening another button on the top of his shirt. I found myself incapable of staring at anything other than the short, curly black hair that was now visible where the button had been clasped and was now open. His chest glistened with the sweat that I felt running down my own neck. I wanted to lick it off him and blow cool air across it. I wanted to taste him.

"Shots or beer?" Kevin asked as he got to the bar and then looked back to us. "My treat."

"Beer," Gavin said. "Something light."

"Pfft, calorie counter," he said. "Lila? Emma?"

"I'll take a beer," Emma said.

"Sure," I said. "Something cold. It's so hot in here."

"What's that? You're super hot? Damn right you are," Kevin said, then elbowed Gavin, his eyebrows waggling. "Right, boss?"

"Huh? Oh. Yes. Yeah," Gavin said. I had never seen him respond to something sheepishly, and it was adorable. His cheeks flushed.

"See? Super hot," Kevin said. "Oh, right. Umm. Four beers, the lightest and coldest you have, please."

The waiter nodded, eyeballing all of us again and then disappearing to the cooler. As she pulled out four longneck beers from the ice, the steam rising off of them, my mouth watered. I hadn't even realized how thirsty I was until that moment.

"Cheers," Kevin said as he handed us the bottles, their tops already opened by the bartender. We clinked glasses, and I took a sip, closing my eyes as the cool liquid hit my tongue.

"Man, that hit the spot," Kevin said, having downed his in one go. "Garçon, one more. No, two more."

"I'm not drinking that fast," Gavin said, laughing.

"Who said I'm ordering it for you?" Kevin laughed back.

"Yeah, who said?" Emma said, then belched. Her hand flew to her mouth, and we all froze. Then a giggle came from deep inside her, matched by the booming laughter of Kevin.

"Make that three," he said, taking her empty bottle.

The bartender obliged, and suddenly the two of them had new beer, Kevin double-fisting his.

"Y'all want to go outside?" Gavin asked. "Get some fresh air?"

"I want to keep dancing," Emma said.

"There's a dance floor outside too," Kevin said. "Come on, little bit. Let's go."

"Little bit?" I asked as the boys went ahead of us and I sidled up to Emma.

She turned to me with a deep smile on her face, her eyes a little glassy.

"He gave me a nickname," she said. "Isn't he just the best?"

"Do you like him?" I asked.

"Lila, I'm five-two. He's like six-nine. He's going to split me in half. *Of course,* I like him."

I laughed audibly as she scampered off ahead of me, finding herself beside Kevin as Gavin slowed down for me to catch up. We walked side by side, our hands brushing each other almost enough to hold hands as we made it outside.

The outdoor dance floor wasn't much cooler than the indoor one as the humidity was pretty high and the summer heat still steamed off the sand. It would cool off as the night wore on, but for now, it was still hot.

We finished our beers, tossing them in a trash can before heading to the dance floor. Only this time, as soon as we were on the checkerboard tile, Gavin pulled me into him and our bodies were crushed together. His hands were on my hips and slowly, as we moved, they trailed up my sides until the tips of his forefinger brushed the bottom of my breast. It might have been accidental. It probably was.

But maybe it wasn't.

I turned, and my chest crushed into his upper stomach, and his abs pressed against me. Our eyes were burning into each other, and slowly, his head began to dip lower. As it did, we stopped moving, stopped dancing. It was happening, and I was powerless to stop it. Our lips cruised closer and closer, and I let my eyes drift shut, fighting myself as much as I was trying to make sure that I enjoyed every single second of what was to come.

Our lips were almost together, the top of his upper lip just brushing the top of mine...

# Chapter Thirteen

## *Gavin*

I WAS PITCHED FORWARD, directly into Lila.

It would have been a perfect, romantic, silly moment, where our lips crushed into each other in a first, accidental kiss, and led to whatever that would lead to afterwards. It would have, had Kevin not been the reason I was pitched forward. Kevin was almost seven feet tall, and it resulted in my forehead smashing into the top of Lila's skull and busting my nose and making her duck away, holding the top of her head.

"What the fuck?" I laughed as I stumbled a few steps away and spun around. "Watch those two left feet, bubba."

"Hey man, chill the fuck out," Kevin was saying to someone else behind him. At first, I thought he was talking to me until I looked over his massive shoulder and caught a glimpse of the man in front of him.

It was the bald-headed biker from the night before.

"Shit," I muttered.

"What the hell?" Lila said, chuckling and rubbing the top of her head.

"We have to go, now," I said, grabbing her hand. If she had resisted, I would have had to leave her there, knowing Kevin would take care of her and the boys weren't there for me anyway. But she didn't resist. She took off behind me without a word, and we ran.

Weaving through the crowd of dancers, we made our way toward the water, where even more people were crowded together. I pulled her behind me through a group of girls, all taking shots and nearly knocking one over as I dove off the raised porch and onto the sand.

Lila shook her hand out of mine, stopping for a moment to take off her heels and then took off behind me as I started running again. Zooming between more people, I looked back over my shoulder. I could see the bald head in the crowd, pushing through like a mob-boss Moses. We were almost to the water now, and I knew I needed to make a choice.

Either I could keep running until either Lila or I was exhausted, and considering the amount she'd had to drink, she was going to get there pretty quickly, or I could try to get her to get safe and fight. I was going to have to. There really wasn't much else I could do.

But for now, I was going to keep running and hope I got us somewhere that they couldn't follow.

"Who are we running from?" Lila panted behind me.

"You don't have to run," I said, turning sharply and heading up the sand toward the far side of the club. Maybe if I could wing around it and back to the street, I could hail a cab or something.

"I'm not letting you run by yourself," she yelled behind me. "I just... oh dammit that hurt... I just want to know what we're running from!"

I glanced back and saw that she had stubbed her toe on the raised platform and was hopping for a moment.

"No time," I said. "Sorry about your foot."

I glanced up and saw the bald head moving through the crowd. They were still down near the water but moving quickly and heading in a long loop this way.

"It's fine," she said, hiccupping. "I'm just not all there, you know. A little more accident prone when I drink tequila, you know? Gavin?"

I was already a few steps away, hoping she wouldn't notice I had taken off while she examined her foot. Instead, she thundered after me, reminding me again that while Lila wasn't tiny, she was fast as hell. She did lead her league in doubles for a reason.

"We just have to keep moving," I said. "I'm sorry."

She groaned and kept running behind me, our feet now back on solid flooring.

"Fine," she said. "Look, that way. I think we can lose them if we go back in the building and out the front."

"Good idea," I said.

Turning hard to head back onto the dance floor, we started making our way back inside. People were still dancing, moving erratically into and out of my way, elbows in my face and blocking my vision. A trickle of blood was running from my nose to the top of my lip, and I brushed it with the back of my hand. My arm glistened red as I looked down at it.

"Oh my goodness," someone said as I passed them. "That guy's bleeding."

I kept moving, not wanting to stop and explain that I had accidentally headbutted the girl behind me because I was being chased by bikers.

The bar was right ahead of us, and I noticed Kevin standing by it. I desperately tried to find a way to get past him without getting close, but people had closed in. There was no other way. At least his back was turned.

"Lila!!!"

Emma's, however, wasn't.

"Shit," I muttered.

"Gavin?" Kevin said, turning toward us. "Hey man, you disappeared on us. Did you see that guy?"

"I did," I said. "Sorry, I have... to go."

"The fuck?" Kevin said.

"There's no time," I said. "I just... I gotta go."

"Hey, you!"

I looked back over Lila's shoulder and saw the bald guy, flanked by two others in jean biker-jackets.

"Shit," I said.

"You need to talk to us," one of them said. "Now."

"That's the guy who ran into me," Kevin said, taking a step between us. "Hey, buddy, what's your problem?"

"Kevin, don't," I said.

"They bothering you?" he asked.

"Gavin, go," Lila said, coming up beside me and pushing at my shoulder. "Kevin can hold them off for a second, and we can get out of here. Then you can tell me what is going on."

"Kev," I said.

"Gavin, meet me back at the hotel. I have some shit to take care of," Kevin said, cracking his knuckles and turning back to the bikers. "Now, you boys, I don't want to have to hurt you, but you are going to want to lower your tone of voice."

"Let's go!" Lila shouted.

Reluctantly, I took off with her, if only to make sure she got to safety too. We flung ourselves through the side door and out onto a sandy area leading to the beach. An Italian ice stand was nearby, and I dragged her toward it. Diving behind it, I stopped to take a breath, Lila pushing her back against the wall and gasping as well. Her shoes were in her hand still, and she set them down on the stand, which apparently had been abandoned for the night.

"If they come out of that door, I have to stand my ground," I said.

"Why?" she thundered. "What the hell is going on? Can you tell me that?"

"It's... it's complicated," I said.

"Try me," she said. When I didn't move or make any indication that I was going to elaborate, she grabbed my shoulder and pulled. Lila was surprisingly strong, and I felt my body wanting to turn toward her anyway. When her eyes locked on to mine, the will to keep her in the dark disappeared. "Gavin, please."

I sighed heavily, looking back at the door again. Whatever Kevin was doing in there was at least keeping them at bay for now.

"I don't tell people about my family," I said. "But this is because of my family."

"What, running from bikers?" she asked. "What the hell is your family into?"

"Everything," I said. "They're into everything. Everything that can get them into massive amounts of trouble, that is."

"Like what?"

"My dad... he's in jail at the moment. He's probably going to prison. He got caught dealing meth, I think. But before he got caught, he did some really, *really* stupid shit."

"Dealing meth is already really stupid shit," she said. "But what did he do specifically?"

"Fair," I said. "He... he owns a bike shop. I worked there sometimes. Anyway, he owned it, and he got into trouble with money and got into business with these guys. At first it was just silly stuff. Low level stuff, right? They would use the backroom to gamble or some shit. Or they would go there to drink and do drugs, but always after hours, right? After the store closed."

"Okay," she said.

"Then it got... worse," I said. "Dad started using again. No one said he did, but I know him. He started using. It's the only way he would have thought he could get away with this. They apparently trusted him, or threatened him, I'm not sure, with hiding a bunch of dope money at the shop. Which, if anyone knows my dad, they know he cannot be trusted with money. Ever. Mom pays what few bills they ever pay. Dad's stupid."

"My mom pays the bills too," Lila said.

"Is your mom also a recovering drug addict, alcoholic, lying piece of shit?"

I could see the forcefulness of what I said hurt her, and I looked away. I didn't want to see how pained those eyes were. Not just from how I snapped at her, but the pity in them. I hated pity. I never wanted to see it in anyone's eyes for me, especially not a girl. Especially not Lila.

"No," she choked out.

"I'm sorry," I said. "I shouldn't snap at you. I'm sorry."

"It's fine," she said, her voice warbling. "But what is going on specifically? What did your dad do?"

"He spent the money," I said.

"He spent the money?"

"He spent it. All of it."

"How much?"

I paused, swallowing hard.

"Twenty thousand dollars," I said. When I looked at her, her jaw was wide and her eyes like quarters. "He spent twenty thousand dollars, and on stupid shit. Some of it on a lawyer after he got popped, I'm sure. Because he showed up at a salon or something that Mom was at, dropped her a couple hundred bucks, and told her to run right before he went back to jail. He must have had bail money and then voluntarily went back in or something. I don't know. All I know is he's missing, and she came here to see me for whatever damn reason. Because I always clean up her mess, probably."

"Oh, Gavin, I had no idea..."

"And now," I said, continuing and hoping to blow right past any platitude of pity, "she's on the road heading south somewhere. And these guys are after me."

"But why you? You don't have anything to do with it," she said, then paused. When she spoke again, her voice was barely above a whisper. "Do you?"

"No," I said firmly. "That's not my life. I barely ever even drink. Tonight was the most I've had in ages. I only ever have anything to drink when Kevin's around, because I don't trust myself, and I know he will take care of me. But even he doesn't know about this."

"Kevin doesn't know about the money?"

"Kevin doesn't know about my *parents*," I said. "I've kept as much as I could from him. I mean, I know he knows some of it. He knows they are pieces of shit. But he doesn't know to what level. I've tried to shield everybody from knowing any of that part of me. Until tonight. Until you."

"Gavin, I..."

"Just... don't," I said. "Look, you don't need to keep running with me. I doubt they even know what you look like. You could saunter down to the beach, and they would never even notice you. They are after me."

"But what for? They don't just expect you to have twenty thousand dollars, do they?"

"Not immediately," I said. "But by next week. And they want a deposit tonight. I told them I would try, but that I didn't know how much I could get because I was busy. I didn't think they'd chase me around, though."

"Shit," she said. "You have a week to come up with twenty grand? What are you going to do?"

I gritted my teeth, my eyes back on the door.

"I don't know. Honestly, Lila, I don't know. But what I do know is Kevin is in there trying to hold them off for me, and he doesn't even know who they are. I should go back in there and straighten it out."

"No," Lila said. "They don't have a beef with him. They're just going to ignore him and come after you. We need to get you somewhere safe."

"But where?" I asked. "I have to be at the hotel for check-in and for the games tomorrow."

# Chapter Fourteen

## *Lila*

I WAS STUNNED. NEVER would I have guessed that Gavin, of all people, would have a home life like that. He seemed so confident, so put together. So perfect.

Of course, there had been signs. He had avoided talking about his family before in conversations. He had spent the holidays mostly on campus, to the point where he hung out with Star and me rather than go home. I probably should have picked up on him not going home as more than a choice of not really wanting to spend time with them like I didn't want to spend time with my folks.

His reasons were much darker. Much more real. My desire not to get picked on because I wasn't waifish thin or because I ate too much at dinner or because I was pursuing sports rather than something more 'pragmatic' seemed wildly childish. My parents didn't accidentally send a biker gang after me to collect money they had blown.

"You said your dad spent it," I said. "Is there any way to get that money back, maybe? Like sell the stuff he bought?"

"I don't think so," he said. "Even if I could get back home and try to sell or return some of it, I probably wouldn't make enough to cover half of it by the end of the week. And that would be giving up the games and everything."

"It's just so unfair," I muttered.

"It's not the first time," he grumbled. "He gambled for a long time. Had a really bad problem with it. Lost a bunch of money and borrowed it from a different biker gang. He used to box and ended up betting on himself and got knocked out. Two for one on that one."

"Oh, shit," I said. "That's horrible."

Gavin simply nodded, his eyes still on the door.

"I had to nurse him back to health with Mom after that fight. Busted eye, busted eardrum, busted brain for all that. He was groggy and clearly had a concussion. And then this dude bust through our door and said Dad owed him five K."

"What did you do?" I asked.

"I was nine. I didn't do shit," he said. "Mom promised we would have it in two days. Then she kissed my head and said everything would be okay and that we needed to pack. We packed all our shit and left Dad there that night. I didn't know what was happening, really, but a couple days later, Dad called us and he somehow worked it out with them. Of course, all our shit was gone in the house. Anything we didn't take with us to the hotel was gone. My bed was gone. My video games. Everything."

"Gavin, that's horrible," I said.

"It's life," he said, shrugging. "But then, that gang got busted for some dumb shit, and Dad started hanging out with a different one. These guys. They're... different. Dad's done boxing now, too old and beat up for it, so he was working on their bikes to get favors, you know? And they routed people to him since he was also doing other shit for them and fixing up their bikes for cheap."

"That's how he ended up dealing?"

"Yup," he said. "He said he only did it occasionally, when they got a bunch of stuff in and needed extra hands to get rid of it. He said he only ever brought it to people who'd already paid, so he wasn't ever in any danger, but he's an idiot, as I have pointed out. He must have gotten popped by an undercover. Why they would let him out on parole, I don't know, but my guess is he's back in now for good. He won't want to show his face to these guys, even if I clean up his mess."

"You can't, though," I said. "You can't just keep fixing things for him."

"I have to," he said. "He's my dad. He's family. I don't have to like it."

"But maybe you could just talk to these guys and explain," I began.

"No," he said, cutting me off. "You don't get it. These guys, they aren't like the other gang he hung out with. They don't want shit they have to sell to get their money back. They want the cash. And they only understand one way of getting it. Violence. And knowing Mom, she said whatever she needed to keep them from getting her. That means she probably told them about my scholarship money."

"Oh no," I said, my hand going to my mouth instinctively. "No, she wouldn't, would she?"

"She would," he said. "She absolutely would if she thought it would buy her a little time. Besides, as far as she's concerned, that's just free money I get, and I can work to pay my college bills. She doesn't get it. She's just waiting around for me to cash a check from a major league team so I can take care of her and Dad for the rest of my life. Like I have ever since I brought home my first check from being a bag-boy at the grocery store."

"What do we do?" I asked.

"*We* don't do anything. You should go. Get out of here. Get somewhere safe. I'll handle this."

"No," I said. "I already told you, I'm making sure you get safe too."

"And that leads us right back to where do we go?" he said, frustrated. "I don't have anywhere."

"Well, the hotel has security guards," I said. "If we can get back there, they can't really do anything once you are on those grounds without getting police involved, right?"

"If they can do something to me to 'convince me' that I need to pay them before security can reach us, they will. They don't care about getting popped and going to jail. One of the other ones will just bail them out, and they will start all over."

"Still, the hotel is the safest place we can be," I said. "Come on. Let's get back there."

"I guess," he said. "If we sneak back this way, we can go around this restaurant and go down the other side of the street." He glanced once more at the door. "Let's go."

Darting across the street, we went around another building and then appeared back on the strip a block later. The club was still visible in the distance, the door we had been watching a small dot on the side of it. Nothing seemed to be happening. Quietly, I wondered what was happening with Emma and Kevin, but figured that Kevin could handle himself, and Emma would have called me by now if something crazy had happened anyway.

Gavin took my hand, and despite everything, I felt a thrill run down my spine when his hand closed over mine. It was silly and stupid, but I liked holding his hand. I liked gripping him as we ran back across the road, only a block from the hotel. The parking lot was nearby, and if we could get into that, we would be in the view of cameras at least.

Just as we made it to the corner of the street, a giant blur nearly ran into us and stopped abruptly. I looked up into the giant face of Kevin, sweat pouring down his forehead and his shirt unbuttoned almost halfway. Emma was behind him, panting and also holding her own heels.

"Gavin, there you are," Kevin said. "I thought you were getting the hell out of there and back to the hotel."

"That's what I'm doing right now," he said. "We waited to see if you were coming with us."

"Well," he said, shrugging and the faintest hint of a smile on his face, "I'm here, boss. I just had a few words I needed to say to some rude fellas back there."

"Oh shit, what did you do?" Gavin asked.

"Nothing," Kevin said, raising his hands in innocence. "I just told them that they knocked into me and made me crush my lady-friend's foot and that she deserved an apology."

"You told them to apologize for you stepping on Emma's foot?" I asked.

Kevin nodded, clearly pleased with himself.

"I did," he said proudly. "And they did."

"Wait, you got them to apologize?" Gavin asked.

"He did," Emma said, curling up to Kevin's arm. "It was very sweet. All three of them said they were sorry and asked to be let past him, but Kevin gave them a good talking to."

"Kev, that has to be the single dumbest thing you have ever done," Gavin said, shaking his head but laughing. "I swear, you are the bravest dummy to walk the planet."

"Thank you," Kevin said, seemingly perfectly fine with that assessment. "Now, do you want to tell me what the hell was going on with you and those terrible dancers?"

"Not particularly," Gavin said.

"Gav, come on, boss," Kevin said.

"It's about Dad," he said.

"Ah," Kevin said, gritting his teeth and looking angrily at the sky as he took a deep breath.

I had seen Kevin put on an angry face on the field before. That was terrifying enough. But the look he was giving the universe in general at that moment was something I would never want me or anyone I cared about to be on the receiving end of. If Kevin had a chance to get to Gavin's father at that moment, I had a feeling Kevin would rip him limb from limb and do it without much effort.

"All right. So you know I need to know exactly what's going on if I can help you," Kevin said. "But that can wait. For right now, we need to get you somewhere safe. Let's get back into the hotel and figure out our options from there."

"They know I'm staying there," Gavin said.

"But there's security and cameras and us," Kevin said, the last of those bringing a warm feeling to my chest. At that moment, we were gathering around Gavin, probably the strongest and most talented person I had ever known, to help him in a moment of need. And Kevin and Emma were doing it without even knowing what was going on.

"That's what I said," I put in. "We were heading there for that reason already."

"Well, good," Kevin said. "At least someone on this team here is thinking. Let's go, boss."

With that, we checked the traffic and headed across the street. The hotel was in sight, and we were almost there. A feeling of safety was beginning to wash over me already as we made our way to the entrance of the parking lot. Then it hit me. When I thought I had seen Gavin in the parking lot before, that really was him. And it was them too. Which meant being on the grounds wasn't a problem for them. We needed to make it inside to be safe.

As we passed under a tall streetlamp, yellow light shone down on our faces. Kevin was grinning, probably feeling safer now, but also probably enjoying the adventure of the night. Emma still had a bit of a glassy look in her eyes, but from what I knew of her, this kind of night was only going to act as lubricant. It was Gavin who didn't look relieved. He knew as well as I did that we weren't safe yet.

Kevin and Emma slowed as we crossed into the parking lot, and I turned to yell to them that we needed to keep up the pace until we were inside. The words were almost out of my mouth when they were stopped by a shove. It came from Gavin, pushing me back into Kevin, who caught me like a bear made of pillows and gently moved me aside.

As my eyes scanned the fast-moving parking lot in the motion of my spin, I saw the three men from the club standing in the shadows. Waiting.

"Gav, look out," Kevin shouted.

Emma screamed.

# Chapter Fifteen

## *Gavin*

AS WE ROUNDED THE CORNER and made it into the parking lot, I knew that they probably thought we were safe. But I knew better. The other day, they'd confronted me right there, right in sight of cameras and people and everything. They didn't care if people saw. They only cared that their message got across.

Passing onto the pavement of the parking lot, Kevin and Emma slowed down, and I skidded to a stop to say something when I noticed what was ahead of me. Three shadowy figures, one of them already moving my way. I shoved Lila toward Kevin and turned to face them, standing on my feet in defiance. One of them, the one that was already moving, was coming around one side, and I braced myself for whatever was going to happen. If it stayed only fists, I had a chance.

A blur passed me, and the sound of two bodies smashing into each other filled the air. I looked down to see Kevin tackling one of them and heard a moan rumble out of him as he was crushed under Kevin's weight. Kevin was already back to his feet, squaring off against one of the others, leaving the bald one for me.

It was on.

I jumped into action, the flurry of punches being swung from me, the bald one, Kevin, and the other guy. I could hear the tell-tale sound of a body losing all its breath as Kevin smashed the other guy in the stomach while I ducked a punch from the bald guy.

One of the few advantages, and there were only a couple, of having my parents was that Dad had taught me to fight at a young age. He was actually a pretty talented boxer when he was young, and I got a good education in how to punch and not hurt myself and how to duck and move.

The bald one's fist sailed over my head as I bobbed to the left and thew out a hook that hit him under the arm. It was an old trick, and one that Dad had taught me early. One of the best ways to win a fight is to take out their arms. They can't punch you if they can't swing. Hitting him under his swinging arm, in the right place, would send a shock to the nerves down his shoulder and arm.

I heard the punch land, and he groaned in pain. I took the chance to step forward, swinging my right elbow into his jaw. He stumbled back and fell on his ass. The first guy was back up, and I heard him running before I saw him. He was heading for Kevin, a lead pipe in one hand. I rushed over, jumping up with my knee and slamming into him. It knocked him off course a few steps as I scrambled back to my feet.

Now he was aiming for me. He was running, holding his pipe up in the air, leaving me with the only options of trying to avoid it or catch it. Neither one was going to work well. I waited until the last possible second to move, and before I did, he suddenly fell forward, crumpling onto the ground. Shocked, I looked up to see Lila, her body in a pitching stance and a heavy rock tumbling on the ground between her and the guy with the pipe.

She had nailed him in the back of the head.

As he lay groaning at my feet, I smiled at her, but she wasn't paying attention. Her eyes had moved to the ground, looking for something else she could launch.

The guy Kevin was fighting had somehow shoved him into the wall and hit him low. Kevin was crumpled, and the guy was taking potshots at his face. Most of them were missing, hitting him in the chest or shoulder, but it was enough to do some damage. I charged at him, knocking him off Kevin and going right into fisticuffs with him.

A blow glanced off my eye, and the blood that had stopped in my nose started again as he doubled up and hit me right on the bridge. It sprayed everywhere, all over my shirt and even onto his. In the flashing light of the overhead streetlamp, I could see him grin.

I went to a knee, but it was on purpose. As he came forward, I launched up and into his stomach, spearing him into the car behind him. An alarm started to sound, and I thought they would leave in a hurry, but it just made it worse.

The bald guy jumped back into the fray, double-teaming me as I tried to fight off the other one. Lead pipe guy was lost somewhere, and I didn't know where he had gone. Kevin was shaking off the blows against the wall, wiping a bit of blood off his cheek, and then he tore toward me, pulling one guy off me with one hand and shoving him away.

I reached up with my legs, wrapping the bald one in a triangle choke and trying to pull him down. His free arm started wailing punches into my thigh, enough to loosen my grip before I could get him down and he was able to wiggle out.

"You motherfucker," he shouted, diving on top of me and sending a right cross over my jaw.

For a moment, everything went dim, bright pinpoint lights flashing in my vision.

But the bald guy was winded, and he tried to catch his breath for a moment as I rolled to my side. He raised his body up and was pelted by something white and heavy that smashed him in the back from Lila's direction.

"Someone get that bitch," the voice of another one said, and I frantically searched for the one with the pipe. I thought he had been knocked out, but now he was gone.

"Touch her and you're dead," I said, kicking at the bald one until he was off of me and I could get to my knee.

"You're the one who's fucking dead, Freeman," the bald one said, rolling to his side and holding his face which was now bleeding. "We told you a deposit. Tonight. And you went dancing. You're a dumb fuck, just like your old man."

"I am *nothing* like him," I said, scrambling over to him and sending a right across his chin. He slumped under me, and I wound back for another. And another. And another.

"Gav!" Kevin's voice shouted behind me, but it was no use. I was seeing red.

"I am *nothing* like him, do you hear me?" I shouted as I rained down shot after shot, aiming for the side of his eye socket. It was another trick I had learned early. If they can't see you, they can't hit you.

Dad had said that.

And now I was on top of another person, hitting them just like he'd taught me. In the spot he taught me.

"Do you hear me?" I roared, stopping the last punch before it fell on him.

There was silence for a moment. I looked up at one of the other men, sitting on his ass between me and Lila, holding his arms over his head as Lila was paused in the pitching position. Kevin was leaning against a car, on one knee. Emma was hiding behind Lila. And a man was below me, mostly unconscious, and his blood was all over my hands.

The blood was on my hands now, I thought. Literally.

This was my problem now.

"Gavin," Kevin said. "I think he gets the point, boss."

"Do you?" I thundered, the anger still searing in my chest like a fiery burning ring of hatred. I hated this. I hated fighting in a parking lot like so many of Dad's own stories. I hated cleaning up his mess. I hated him.

I hated myself.

"Yes," the crumpled, bloody mass of a human below me said. "Just get off me."

"You get the fucking point?" I thundered again, unsatisfied. "I am not my father. You want something from him, you get it from fucking him. I don't pay his bills. Got it?" I grabbed the shirt of the man below me and shook, his limp head scraping the concrete below. "Got it?"

"Yes," he spat, blood coming from his lips and hitting my chin. "I got it."

"Now get the fuck out of here," I said.

Slowly, I stood, still not trusting him. He crawled a few feet, meeting the other one halfway and looking back.

"You got spirit, kid," the bald one said. "You're right. You aren't like your old man. You're a better fighter than he is."

"I don't care," I said. "Just go. Get out of here. And leave me and my friends alone."

"Sure, sure," he said, getting to his feet. He shot off a mock salute, grinning with a mouth full of broken teeth. "Just one more thing."

"What?" I asked.

"You're right-handed, right?"

I scrunched up my face in confusion. What kind of question was that?

"Yeah," I said, opening my mouth to say something else.

"GAVIN!" Kevin's voice boomed.

But it was too late. The entirety of all sound in my mind was filled with the crunch of a lead pipe crushing into my right shoulder. It felt like someone had sawn it off, and yet the nerves were still out, being tortured while the arm hung limply. I cried out in pain and went down to a knee. The person behind me clearly thought I was done, and in a last bit of anger, a last bit of fury, I jumped up, smashing the top of my head into his chin.

He went down below me as I fell with the momentum on top of him. He was out cold. The pipe clanged on the ground and rolled under a car as I went onto my back, holding my limp arm to my side.

"Fucking hell," Kevin said. "Get out of here, now! Now!"

The bald one and the other ran forward, looking cautiously at Kevin and back at Lila, who now had a selection of heavy things to fling. They looped the unconscious pipe-swinger's arms over their shoulders and began to hurry out. The bald one was laughing.

"Fuck, fuck, fuck," I muttered, pushing my back against a car as Kevin stepped between me and the fleeing bikers.

I heard the clatter of rocks hitting the ground, and suddenly Lila was beside me. She knelt down, and I watched as her eyes roamed all around me, unsure of what injury to pay attention to most. Or first. I was sure there was a lot of them.

"Your arm!" Emma said, joining her. "Oh shit, your pitching arm!"

"They're gone," Kevin said. "At least for now. Let's get inside." He turned toward me, and our eyes met after he got a look at my arm. "Oh fuck, Gav, that's not good. That's really not good."

"I know," I said. "It hurts like hell."

"I fucking bet," he said. "Let's get you inside."

"To my room," Lila said, interrupting us. "Get him to my room. They don't know me, and they don't know what room I'm staying in. Come on."

"Good call," Kevin said. "Bro, can you walk?"

"My legs are fine," I said. "I just need help getting up."

Kevin reached down and hooked his giant hand in my belt buckle and looked me direct in the eyes.

"On three. One. Two. Three."

He pulled, and I straightened my legs. Kevin got me to my feet in one tug.

"Thanks, buddy," I said. "I'm sorry."

"Don't you fucking dare," he said. "I'd do this for you any day of the week, seven times a week, you know that."

"Let's go in the side door," Emma said, rushing ahead of us. "If we walk in the lobby, people will have questions I'm not sure you want to answer."

"Smart," I said, trying to ignore the pain. "Lila, can you go with her and just make sure we have a clear path to the stairwell and then to your room?"

"Done," she said, rushing ahead. "Kevin, I'll wave you in."

"Got it," he said.

With that, they rushed inside, and I leaned my good arm against the wall. Blood smeared on it from my forehead, and I groaned.

Then Kevin laughed. And laughed and laughed. It got louder and heavier, and as I turned my face toward him in frustration and horror, I found to my shock that I was laughing too.

"Son of a bitch," he said. "Son of a bitch that was a scrap."

# Chapter Sixteen

## *Lila*

KEVIN WAS STANDING by the window as Emma and I helped Gavin to the bed. We laid him down gently, but his arm was clearly in a tremendous amount of pain. Not to mention the bruises and scrapes and cuts that rumbling with those large men had brought. A slice that ran down his eyebrow and part of his cheek was still bleeding, though by the time we got back to the room, it wasn't nearly as bad as it had been. His eye was starting to swell, though.

"How bad does it look?" he asked as I gently wiped dirt and blood from his cheek and examined the cut.

"It's not great," I said. "Not going to lie, that's going to hurt for a while."

"Figured," he said. "Way more worried about my arm, though."

"Me too," I said.

"So tell me why we came here, exactly," Kevin said, peering through the curtain that was drawn over my room's window.

"They don't know me," I said. "They don't know who I am or what room to look for me in. If they decided to come into the hotel, they would look for him in his room. This is safer."

"Fair enough," he says. "It looks like they kind of collapsed out on the street a half block down."

"Let me see," I said, moving to the window beside him.

Sure enough, all three men were leaning against the side of a building a little way down the road. It was hard to see them at first because they were sitting in shadows, but eventually, a flash of a car headlight lit them up. One was standing, bent at the waist like he was breathing heavily, the bald one was sitting on the ground, his head rested against the wall, and the other one, the one with the tire iron, had his head in his hands and was seated with his legs splayed out in front of him.

"They look like they regret the fight a bit," Kevin smirked. "We really worked them over, boss."

"They worked us over too," Gavin said. "I don't think I'm going to be able to pitch tomorrow."

"Yeah, I don't see that happening," Emma said. "Not with that arm."

"Maybe I can be suddenly ambidextrous?" Gavin laughed, then moaned. The pain was probably starting to worsen now that the adrenaline was wearing off.

"I mean, you can try," Kevin said. "You hit from both sides as it is. Maybe you'll have better control of your curve from the left-hand side."

"Har, har," Gavin said. "Shit, this really hurts. Like a lot."

I crossed over to him, still bothered by the story about what was going on. Something just didn't make sense. If the biker guys wanted Gavin to pay up, wouldn't they make sure he had the ability to do so? Why ruin his scholarship if that was the way he was going to be able to make the money? If they really messed up his shoulder, he'd be out of school and out of money.

"What's wrong?" Gavin asked when he saw my face. I glanced at Kevin and Emma, who were now both looking out of the window together.

"I just... I don't get it."

"Get what?" he asked.

"Why they would do this. Especially if they said you had a week. Why attack you?"

He sighed.

"These aren't rational people," he said. "They don't operate with logic. They want their money. They want it now. If they see me doing anything, and I mean anything, that doesn't directly result in making that money, they think I don't take them seriously."

"That's ridiculous," I said, shaking my head.

"They don't deal with rational people, either. My dad is not a rational person. He would absolutely tell them he is going to get them money and then go directly to a casino or a club and blow more of it. This is what they are used to. And if they caught him doing it, they'd do much worse to him than what happened to me. Because he doesn't have friends."

He glanced over at Kevin, who nodded solemnly back.

"You know I've got your back," he said. "Always, boss."

"I know," Gavin said. "And it makes me feel like shit that you had to step in tonight. Because none of this should be on me. This is my dad's mess that I have to clean up now."

He tried to sit up on the bed and immediately fell back, howling in pain.

"Your shoulder?" Kevin asked.

Gavin nodded.

"He needs a doctor," Kevin said. "Like, now."

"No," Gavin said. "If this gets out, I'm put on the IL, and if I'm on the IL, it's ten days minimum. I won't be in any of the games."

"Dude, you won't be any good in any of the games anyway. Your shoulder's fucked," Kevin said.

"I think it's dislocated," he said. "It just needs to be reset. I just need someone who knows how."

"What if we called Katie?" Emma asked.

Everyone in the room turned to her.

"Katie?" Gavin asked.

"Katie Pepper," I said. "She's our team doctor. She's also really close with Emma's family."

"She and my sister grew up together," Emma said. "I bet she'd keep a secret if we asked her to."

"Call her," Kevin said.

"No," Gavin interrupted, but Kevin shook him off.

"Boss, I am doing this for you. You don't get a say. Call her. If she can't or won't, you're going to our team doc and the chips fall where they may. I'll back you up on whatever you want to tell them, but you need to see someone," Kevin said.

"What do we tell her?" Emma asked. "I hate lying to her."

"We don't lie," Gavin said. "We were at a club, some guys got handsy, it got rough in the parking lot, and one of them hit me in the shoulder with a tire iron."

"That's... a simplified version of what happened," I said.

"It's the truth. Just missing some details. Call her. See if she can come over tonight. This hurts like a motherfucker."

"Do it," I said, looking to Emma, who nodded and pulled out her phone.

"Hey, Katie," she said into it, walking into the little bathroom area. I could still hear her clearly. Kevin continued to monitor the window as I grabbed a bottled water and opened it, tipping it back so Gavin could get some. "Yeah, so, I need a really big favor. Like massive big. Like family big. Can you come over to room 316? Quietly?"

A few moments later, a light knock on the door indicated she had arrived. When Emma opened the door, Katie smiled, gave her a hug, then she saw Gavin, and her face went from happy to shocked.

"Oh shit, what happened?" she asked. "Gavin?"

"Hey," he said. "Sorry, I don't think we've formally met."

"Not really," Katie said, coming over to the side of the bed. I could see her eyes going up and down Gavin's various wounds, but they always came back to his shoulder. "We met once or twice, but it was in passing."

"Ah, well, nice to really meet you," he said. "So I kind of have a situation."

"I'll say," Katie said. "What the fuck happened?"

"They got jumped," Emma said, completely honestly. "Some guys got handsy at the club we went to and when we got back to our hotel, they were waiting for us. Kevin and Gavin defended us all."

"You should see the other guys," Kevin said, no longer watching through the window, lest he raise suspicion.

"I bet," Katie said, looking Kevin up and down. "But Gavin, it looks like you did a number on your shoulder here."

"They hit me with a tire iron," he said. "I think it's dislocated."

"Hmm," she said, coming around to that side and making me move out of her way. "Do you mind if I get your shirt off? As much as you can, at least."

"No, that's fine," Gavin said. "I just... I might need some help."

"I've got it," I said, jumping into action perhaps a little more enthusiastically than was entirely necessary. I helped open the buttons on the rest of his shirt, doing my best not to stare directly at his stomach, and then peeled it out and over his still-functional left shoulder. Then he sat up, and I stuffed it behind him so Katie could get it off his right, very gently.

"There we go," she said.

There were a few minutes where she looked over his various injuries and then sighed.

"That bad?" Gavin asked.

"That bad," she said. "I'm assuming you called me as a favor because you want to see if you can get this all fixed without getting your coach involved."

"That was my idea," Emma said. "Sorry, Katie."

"It's fine," Katie said. "I mean, no, it's not fine, and I am extremely disappointed, but I won't tell anyone. But here's the problem. I think your shoulder is dislocated, but if I push it back in, it's going to hurt like hell for a second. And after that, it will be sore for a week or two. You probably won't be able to pitch with it during that time. Not effectively and not without risking injury, that is."

"Shit," he said.

"Yeah," she continued. "Let me go back to my room and get some stuff. I'll be back in about ten minutes, okay? You just stay here."

Gavin nodded as she got up and headed for the door. As she went out, Kevin checked one last time out of the window and sighed.

"I think they're gone," he said. "I don't see them anymore over there, and I don't think they're going to come back for round two tonight."

"What if they come back to shoot us?" Emma said, clinging to Kevin's arm. He patted her sweetly on the back of her hand.

"Not their style," Gavin said. "They aren't a shooting type gang. Not unless it's the last resort scenario. They send messages through jumping people or shooting up a house, but not straight murder in a hotel room."

"Still," Kevin said, "I don't think it's a good idea for you to go back to your room tonight."

"That's why he's staying here," I said. "With me."

"Oh," Gavin said.

"Oh," Kevin said.

"Ohh..." Emma said.

There was far more to hers than the others', and I wasn't happy about it.

"I guess that makes sense," Gavin said. "Kev, could you bring me some clothes and stuff from my room?"

"Sure, boss," he said.

"Are you going to keep an eye on his room tonight?" Emma asked, and I could sense the hidden question inside it. Kevin looked like he wasn't sure if she was asking what he thought she was but was willing to find out.

"Well... I thought... it might be a good idea..."

"You shouldn't be alone either," Emma said immediately. "Why don't I stay with you, and we can take turns keeping an eye on Gavin's room. Since Gavin's going to be here with Lila and all..."

She shot a look at me that I wasn't entirely sure was conspiratorial, but I had a very, *very* good feeling was.

"Sure..." Kevin said, still not completely picking up on the giant neon signs that Emma was turning on. "You all right with that, boss?"

"Yeah, I'll be fine. Me and Lila are cool. She owes me one anyway." He turned his head slightly toward me, wincing as he did, and grinned.

I felt like my stomach was suddenly full of bees.

"Why's that?" Kevin said, still not picking up on Emma or really anything else going on in the room. He might have been an incredibly intelligent and sensitive giant, but he was a little dim when it came to picking up on signals sometimes.

"I was sick," I said. "He came over to help take care of me. Spent a bunch of time making sure I didn't puke my guts out."

"Gross," Emma said.

"Yeah, well, getting sick sucks," I said.

"Well, you can do all that then. We're going to head on up to Kevin's room," Emma said, then turned to him and lowered her voice a little. "Hey, do you mind if we stop by my room for a minute? Let me grab some stuff."

"Sure," he said. "I probably have anything you'd need, though. I went to the little grocery store down there and got some ramen and..."

"I meant like clothes. And other... things."

"Oh, I mean I have some sweaters and stuff if you get cold," Kevin continued, still not getting it.

"That's nice," Emma said, stroking his arm in a motion that screamed horny frustration. "I just have a couple other things I'd like to bring up. Say, what's your favorite color between red and black?"

"Me? My favorite color is yellow, but..."

"Yes, but between red and black?"

"Uhh... red, I think," he said. "I like them both."

"Good," Emma said. "I like both too."

As their conversation continued, they left the room, briefly leaving Gavin and me alone for the first time since we had peeled off at the club.

"They're going to fuck, aren't they?" Gavin asked.

"If Emma has anything to say about it, yes," I laughed. "Maybe not if he doesn't figure it out, though."

"Oh, he will figure it out eventually," Gavin said. "She was practically peeling her clothes off by the door."

"Yes, she was," I said. "That's Emma, though. She's not particularly shy around people she likes."

"People?"

"Mmm-hmm," I said.

"Oh, then they're going to get along *splendidly*," Gavin laughed.

"Oh," I said, then my eyes widened. "Oh!"

"Anyway, I'm sorry your only night of fun ended up babysitting me and my jacked-up arm," he said. His eyes went to his shoulder, but mine were magnetically attracted to his chest. His stomach. The deep V-shape that led into his pants. It was the first time I had seen him shirtless, and it was driving me absolutely insane.

"Oh, no problem," I choked out. "Seriously. I owe you. This is... this is just fine. Can I get you something to drink?"

"No," he said. "I want to wait on Katie to get back. Figure out what I need to do."

"Sure, sure," I said, suddenly remembering that another person was going to burst this tiny, intimate bubble soon. I hated it. I wanted him all to myself.

Of course, that was a silly thought. He wasn't mine to have, was he?

I swallowed that thought as fast as I could. There was no reason for any of that. It was just going to make things more difficult.

A knock on the door broke my train of thought, and I got up to open it. Katie swept in carrying a satchel and glanced around her.

"Just you two? Where's Emma?"

"She decided to go hang out with Kevin for a bit," I said.

"He the giant?" she asked.

"Yup," I said.

"Sounds like Emma," she muttered under her breath. "Been boy crazy since she was twelve. Likes 'em tall. Not usually *that* tall, but, hey."

"So what do I need to do, Doc?" Gavin asked.

"Well, for one thing, don't call me 'Doc,' okay?" she asked. "It makes me sound like a character in a Bugs Bunny cartoon. I'm Katie. You can call me that. I'm only like three years older than you."

"Really?" I asked.

"Yes," she said. "Technically I am the team physician, but I am still in medical school. I have classes just like you guys."

"Oh," I said. "I had no idea."

"Neither does Emma," she said, smiling. "I'll be honest, if it weren't for softball, that girl wouldn't be here. She's only in higher education to get her M.R.S. degree. It's a disgrace to womankind, if you ask me."

I laughed.

"M.R.S.?" Gavin asked.

"Think about it," Katie said. "Just take all the time you need. Meanwhile, hold out your arm by your side. Just like that. Now look to your left, and..."

There was a loud crack. Gavin started to make a howling sound and suddenly stopped.

"Hey! Hey… that worked! Oh shit, it's sore as hell, but it worked!"

"Yup," Katie said. "Now, you're going to need something for pain, but I am not about to give you anything harder than Tylenol. If you want to see your own team doc and get something from him, that's not my business, but leave my name out of it, okay?"

"Got it," Gavin said.

"As for this mouse under your eye, the cuts and bruises… I don't know what to tell you. It's going to hurt. And you're going to have a hell of a shiner in the morning. Good luck explaining that to your coach. Until then, I'd take two of those, once every four hours, drink water, no alcohol, and try to get some rest. Ice your eye. Now, if you will excuse me…" She stood up. "What room is Kevin in? I just so happen to have a pack of condoms in my bag, and I might find myself accidentally tripping and letting them slide under his door."

"What about pitching?" Gavin asked.

She shook her head slowly.

"Sorry, Gavin. I don't see that happening."

# Chapter Seventeen

## *Gavin*

MY HEART SANK.

Resetting my arm had worked so perfectly, I was sure it meant that I would be fine. Maybe not tomorrow, sure, but the next day? By the weekend? I had so much hope. But the way Katie looked at me when I asked, it felt like the thought was way out of the realm of possibility.

"Ah," I said.

"Sorry," she said again, packing her things.

"I mean, I could try though, right?" I asked. "If I'm feeling better and my arm isn't too sore? Like maybe not tomorrow but the next day?"

She stopped packing and looked at me sadly. Her lips were pursed as she glanced at Lila and then me, as if judging what our relationship was. Then she patted my hand softly.

"You could, theoretically," she said, "but I wouldn't get your hopes up. The issue is that it might have been more damage than we know. You will want to get seen by a doctor who can do an x-ray, take some images. Maybe an MRI. You could have torn tendons, muscles, who knows. You said you got hit by a tire iron?"

"Yes," I said.

"Gavin, that could have done a lot more damage than you think. You still have adrenaline in your system right now. It will take several hours to dump all that out, and then, the pain that you are feeling currently might seem like a walk in the park comparatively. You need to be prepared for waking up in the morning and feeling like your shoulder is made of stone. Or like someone is pushing a rod up your arm and over your shoulder every time you move."

"But if it doesn't feel like that," I said, "if it's not all that bad feeling, I could give it a shot, right?"

"That's up to you, I suppose," she said, sighing. "And your coach. You have to tell your coach. They need to know if they are putting you in injured, though with how swollen your face is, I don't see that being something they could miss. But you need to be honest about this. If you are hurt in a way we can't tell, and you throw a pitch in just the right way, you could tear your rotator cuff or any of the muscles in and around the upper arm. You might overcompensate and tweak your elbow. You might develop a career-ending injury just trying to force yourself to pitch after this rather than healing up. I really do think you should rest and not pitch this week."

"Thank you," he said. "I appreciate you helping us."

"Sure," she said. "But again, you never saw me. If anyone asks, I came to see my best friend's sister, who was hanging out here."

"Got it," Gavin said.

With that, Katie stood up and headed toward the door. She stopped with her fingers on the knob.

"Do you guys need anything?" she asked. "I have some extra..."

"No," Lila said. "We're fine."

"Okay," Katie said, a thin smile on her face. "All right then. Good luck, Gavin."

"Thank you," Lila and I chorused as she shut the door behind her.

"Well, that sucks. A lot," I said.

"I'm sorry," Lila said. "I can't imagine how awful you must feel. On top of just the pain and everything. I thought I was going to lose it just being sick and missing practices. Missing the games is awful. I wish there was something I could do for you."

"I appreciate it, Lila. I do," I said. "But I should probably let you have your room back. My legs are fine, I can walk up to my room."

"I mean, you don't have to," she said, and there was something in that voice, almost to the edge of pleading.

"I wouldn't mind staying," I said. "If you really were okay with it."

"Absolutely," she said. "You can take the bed, even."

"Oh, no, I couldn't do that," I began.

"No, seriously, take the bed. I've been in it way too much this week, and the couch is plenty big for me. You were adorable all crunched up on there, but I fit perfectly, and I don't mind. I insist."

"All right," I said. "If you insist. But only if we watch that baking show again. That was funny."

A warm-looking blush crossed her face, and she smiled.

"I'd love to," she said. "Hey, do you think room service is still going?"

"Maybe," I mused. "What time is it?"

"Ooh, probably not," Lila said. "It's almost two."

"Shit," I said. "Well, that settles that."

"Not so fast," she said, grinning. She ran over to the little mini-fridge under the television and popped it open. From inside, she drew out two sandwiches and a couple cans of soda.

"What the hell?" I laughed.

"Remember when I said Coach bought dinner for everyone?" she asked. "Well, before we went outside to eat, I brought a couple sandwiches up here, just in case. I'm rather frugal, and free is free."

I laughed.

"I am similarly frugal when it comes to free food," I said. "What kind are they?"

I felt myself sinking into a familiar feeling, one that didn't quite fit the scenario we were actually in. I was broken, my body beat up and slowly scabbing over, one eye getting closer to swollen shut with each passing second. I was still feeling the effects of punches and kicks to my head and body and was lying shirtless in someone else's bed, probably bleeding on it.

Yet, Lila and I had a chemistry, a rhythm. When I was her tutor, it made it easy for us to interact, for me to teach her because we seemed to understand each other beyond language. After that, it made it so much less awkward when I would come ostensibly to hang out with Star, who was often completely busy with whatever project she was working on.

Now we were alone, in a hotel room, and I was shirtless after a fight where she'd helped me by tossing heavy rocks at people with a pitch speed that was extraordinarily dangerous. And yet, we were acting like Star was on the floor, putting glued pieces of cotton on a project or covering her forearm in paint to use it exclusively to create something she called "ForeArt."

But Star wasn't there. She was in France. Doing... whatever.

"Gavin?" Lila asked, and I realized I had drifted off into a train of thought and not heard her when she was talking.

"Oh, sorry. What was that?"

"Turkey and Swiss or ham and Cheddar," she said. "Which one?"

"Whichever you don't want," I said. "I'm good either way."

"Turkey and Swiss then," she said, handing me the sandwich. "I've honestly been thinking about this ham and Cheddar sandwich since I put it in the fridge."

"Even while we were out dancing?" I laughed.

"Even while we were out dancing," she confirmed. "I kind of love ham."

"I remember at Thanksgiving that being a thing. You said ham was superior to turkey."

"It is," she said.

"Not at Thanksgiving, though," I said.

"At any time," she teased. "Ham is superior."

"Nuh-uh," I said.

"You're wrong," she laughed, opening her sandwich and nearly salivating. "Believe it."

I laughed and took a bite of the turkey and Swiss. I didn't realize until just that moment how hungry I had gotten. The combination of the dancing, the alcohol, and the fight had worked up one hell of an appetite. I could probably put away several of these sandwiches without an issue.

I tried to keep it slow and savor it instead. I didn't want to eat too quickly, but I also just enjoyed the act of eating with Lila. It was an intimate thing to eat with someone, even if you weren't looking at each other. There was something carnal about it, about putting food in your mouth, about sustaining your body. About licking your lips and occasionally making those tiny moans of appreciation.

The hair on the back of my neck stood up.

Then it hit me. We should probably call Star.

"Hey, so, I should probably call Star," I said.

"Oh, yeah, you probably should," she said, keeping her eyes down on her sandwich and nodding. "Might be a good idea to give her a head's up that your eye looks like a ripe olive at the moment."

I laughed.

"That bad, eh?"

"The purple is starting to show up," she said. "It's going to look pretty rough in a little while."

"Well, then no time to waste, I guess," I said. "Once we're done with our snack, I think I should give her a call."

"Do you want me to leave?" she asked. "So you can have some privacy?"

"No," I said. "She might like to see you."

"Okay," she said, looking unconvinced.

I made a mental note to put on some form of shirt before the call and continued eating my sandwich. As I neared the last few bites, my jaw began to ache. It was a harbinger of soreness to come, I was sure. I was looking forward to a long week of pain. And still no idea if there was more of it on the way.

That was what scared me most, really. That they weren't done. And it wasn't even about me. Them jumping me was what it was. I would handle that. But if they cornered Lila...

I tried to shake it off. That kind of fear wasn't going to help anyone. We just needed to all be vigilant, and while I was sure Kevin was rather distracted at the moment, he was also going to be more observant than most people would. Because it was important to me. I trusted Kevin, and he didn't take that trust lightly, and after tonight, he had a bone to pick too. He wasn't just going to let these guys sneak up on any of us.

"She never did respond to our text," I said, as I pulled the phone over to me. "What time is it over there again?"

"Eight, I think. Or almost eight," she said. "Morning, at any rate."

"That might be the problem. She might be asleep," I said. "You think it's worth calling her?"

Lila shrugged. She seemed uncomfortable with the idea. I wondered why.

I hit her contact number and pressed the call button. She had seen my text. She just hadn't responded. Maybe she just got up.

The phone rang three times before it was finally answered, and the sound from the other side was loud enough to make me pull the phone away from my ear.

"Sheesh" Lily said from on the couch. "That's super loud."

"Star?" I asked. "Are you there?"

A voice shouted something muffled. It was deep, like a guy, and then Star's voice responded.

"Hold on," she shouted.

A notification came up on the phone, and as I stared at it, I realized it was a request to turn the call into a video call. I hit OK and waited. The screen went black, and the sound came back full force. I could hear that it was music, loud and thumping, with indistinct voices in the background. Star was saying something, but it was impossible to hear her, and aside from what I assumed were glowsticks around her neck, I couldn't see her either.

"I can't see you or hear you," I said. "Star, can you hear me?"

"Yes!" her voice shouted, then more mumbling that I couldn't understand.

I looked over at Lila, who was standing now, heading my way. She shrugged, and I looked back at the phone.

Suddenly, light filled the screen, and the next thing I saw was a bathroom stall. She had gone into what looked a lot like a club bathroom. Graffiti was on the walls and on the stall door, and Star looked down into the phone as she seemingly leaned against the sink counter. The reflection behind her showed she was wearing a mesh shirt. I couldn't see anything under it either.

"Star?" I asked.

"Gavin? I can barely hear you. What's up?"

"Where are you?" I asked, and the look that crossed her face was one of both annoyance and frustration.

"France," she said. "You knew that."

"No, I meant where are you right now? I thought it was like eight in the morning there?"

"Is it?" she said, then shrugged. "It's a club. They don't *do* closing times in Paris. Not the clubs at least. You can order drinks all night in this place."

Almost as an exclamation point, she brought a drink to her lips and sipped on the straw. The bright, neon blue drink slowly disappeared.

"Oh, cool," I said. "I didn't want to bother you, but I thought you might want to know. I got jumped tonight."

"You jumped?" she asked, looking slightly inebriated and thoroughly distracted. She kept looking off camera, like she was watching the door. "What now?"

"I said I was jumped. I'm in Lila's room. She's taking care of me because I got attacked by some dudes out here. They cracked my shoulder pretty bad."

"Oh. Hi, Lila," Star said.

"Hi," Lila said, putting her head into frame. I realized at that moment I hadn't put the shirt on, but it didn't seem to matter to Star. She was completely unfazed by anything I had told her so far.

"I might not be able to pitch this week. It's a really big problem."

"That sounds like a bummer," Star said. "Sorry to hear that. Hey, did you make sure to turn off all the lights at the apartment, Lila? I didn't turn anything off when I left, and I don't want people thinking I'm home and coming by and getting upset when I don't answer the door. You know how people are."

For the first time in the conversation, she seemed to smile. Because she was talking about herself. And how other people cared so much about her they'd be upset if they didn't hear from her.

"I did," Lila said, the slight exasperation in her voice telling me that she knew long ago that it would be her job to make sure things like that were done.

"Good," Star said. "Oh, shit, hey, can you send my mom a text? Just tell her I'm good. She won't be up until like eleven, and I will be asleep by then. I know she's texted me three or four times, but I keep getting distracted."

"You haven't told your mom you're okay?" I asked.

Star shrugged again.

"She knows I went to France. Time difference. All that. Anyway."

"Yeah, anyway," I said. "So, yeah, I'm probably going to hang out here tonight. If I'm not going to pitch this week…"

"Cool. Have fun. I have to go," Star interrupted. "I'll call you guys when I land, see which one of you is going to pick me up. Ciao!"

And with that, the screen went blank. I stared at it for a second, not believing what I had heard and seen.

She didn't even care. Not only did she not care that I wasn't going to pitch, which I might be able to overlook since she knew absolutely nothing about baseball, but she didn't seem to care about me looking like someone had shoved cotton under one of my eyes and then painted it black. Or that I was shirtless in Lila's bed.

Nothing.

"Are you okay?" Lila asked.

"No," I said. I didn't want to be dishonest. That hurt. Maybe even worse than my face right now, that hurt. I had been trying like hell all this time to not do anything that would make me feel guilty, tearing myself apart over the feelings I was having toward Lila, and then she did this?

"I tried to warn you about Star," she said. "This is who she is. She's a sweet girl, but she is a self-centered person. It's difficult to be her friend sometimes. I can only imagine how hard it is to be a boyfriend to her."

I muttered something under my breath, something that came from a deep place inside my chest and forced its way out without bothering to check with my brain if it was okay. A phrase that had a ton of meaning and if it was said aloud might alter how I handled things going forward. A thought that was buried deep under the guilt of how I had used Lila to get close to Star, how I had pined after her, how I had done everything I could to transition into being a good boyfriend, and how much work I had put into our budding relationship.

How I had planned this whole trip so differently.

And how I was kind of glad it was working out the way it was. Bruises, busted arm, blood, and all.

"What was that?" Lila asked. There was apprehension in her voice, almost like she didn't know if she wanted to know for sure what I said.

Then I realized, fully, what I had said.

Out loud.

To Lila.

There was no going back now.

# Chapter Eighteen

## *Lila*

"I DON'T THINK SHE'S my girlfriend anymore," he said.

I had stared at him for a moment, trying to determine if I'd heard him correctly, and when I asked him to repeat it, he did. But he looked like he was just realizing what he said as he said it. Like it had come from a deep place inside him and surprised even himself.

Then he nodded, seemingly accepting it.

"Yeah," he said. "I think that's it. I think... I think I'm breaking up with her."

"What?" I asked, my heart thumping in my chest. A weird sense of panic was running through me, and I wasn't entirely sure why.

"I just... I was so enamored with her when we met, right? She was so pretty and so ... weird. I just was blown away by her. And I interpreted that as being head over heels for her."

"That's not the first time I've heard her described like that," I said. "But none of them got to her like you did."

"But that was because of you," he said. "She is so self-centered, so concerned with whatever it is that makes her happy right that moment that she doesn't think about *anybody* for more than five minutes. She only thought about me because I was around you all the time and I was unavoidable. That's how we planned it, remember?"

I nodded. He was right. We'd essentially run a modified Pavlov experiment on her by having Gavin with me all the time, until she associated him with being comfortable, and then let him hit on her. And at first, I had been all for it. So had he.

"I do," I said.

"But it was stupid," he said. "Because it wasn't real. None of it was real. The second she was no longer in her routine of seeing me, I became invisible. The damn second."

He was getting upset, and I didn't know if I should try to calm him or let him let it out. Part of me thought letting him get angry like this might just make his current situation worse. And as his friend, I wanted him to be comfortable and calm while he tried to rest through all the injuries. But another part of me, a not-so-secret part of me anymore, wanted to hear what he had to say. It wanted to hear that he wasn't enamored with Star anymore. That the spell was broken.

That there was a chance.

Then again, there was part of me that wanted to defend my friend. Star had been my friend since we met. She had been sweet and nice to me when she didn't have to be, and while everything he said was true, and was part of the difficulties of being Star's friend, it wasn't like Star ever pretended to be anything she wasn't. She was upfront about herself, as much as she could be without actually doing any introspection. She was a walking, talking 'beware' sign, and if you ignored it, that was on you.

I vacillated between the various mixed emotions like a furiously played tennis match. She was my friend. He was my friend. Yet, if he was single and I was single...

I had to get that off my mind. I had to let it go completely. He was just angry with her, and with good reason, because she was far away and not seeming terribly interested in anything other than what she was up to. Once she was back in physical touch again, once he could see her deep, fetching eyes and touch her tiny, tight body, he was going to forgive her.

Everyone forgave her.

Including me.

I needed to let go of any idea that Gavin was going to be single. He wasn't. He was going to be angry, maybe even do something stupid and rash while at the beach, and then go home and forget it ever happened and get back with Star. And they would be happy together, both knowing the other was probably up to no good and neither one caring because that's what beautiful people did.

I just had to keep my name out of it. I needed to keep far enough away that I wasn't going to be the one who got used to get back at her. And I needed to keep my heart in a locked box, so it didn't get hurt by lifting it up and then letting it go crashing down when this week was over.

"I'm sorry," Gavin said. "I don't mean to blow up around you. I'm just very angry. And confused. I have a lot to think about, not the least of which is what I'm going to tell Coach in the morning."

"Yeesh, yeah," I said, happy to move on to a different subject. Something with less potential to end with me telling him that if he wanted to get over Star, that I was currently fighting the effort to not remove all my clothes and tell him to take it out on me, and all I needed was literally one word from him.

Just one word.

"I know I'm not the first guy on the team to get into a bar fight before a game," he said casually. "I remember my first year on the team... Jason? I think his name was Jason. He was the first baseman. Anyway, he got into it with one of the guys on another team during a tournament week, and they beat the shit out of each other. Both of them ended up playing against each other the next day and were fine. Coach just let them go."

"Wow," I said. "You would think the school would step in."

"Not for us," he said. "Our school makes so much money off sports that they just kind of let the coaches handle things internally without interference. Especially if it's football, but apparently with baseball too.

But this year, he's been... distracted a bit. I'm worried he might want to make an example of me to kind of get control of the locker room again."

"Oh," I said, nodding. What he was saying was interesting. It's just that I didn't care. I couldn't care. Not when the words he said about Star were still ringing in my ears. The potential for what it meant was still heavy on my chest, crushing down on me like an elephant.

"Anyway, I can't worry myself too much about it now," he said. "I need to just focus on getting some rest tonight and getting down there early tomorrow. Do you know what time you need to be down on the fields?"

"Hmm?" I asked, then the words caught up in my mind, and I shook my head and smiled. "Eleven. We don't start practice until eleven tomorrow."

"Late start. Interesting. Are you okay?"

I wanted to tell him so badly. I wanted to tell him how I wanted him. How I felt like I needed him. How that feeling had just grown and grown over the last few days, and after dancing at the club, I was pushed beyond my limit to control it. The way his body had molded into mine, how I could feel his hardened cock against my thigh when we danced. The way our eyes met and I was absolutely sure we were going to kiss before Kevin barreled into us.

It was all there, right on the tip of my tongue. I wanted to tell him that when I was throwing those rocks, I wasn't just joining in the fray. I was trying to specifically get them off him. I wanted to protect him, even at the cost of my own well-being. How that wasn't just lust. How that wasn't just jealousy. How that was something deep inside me that had been brewing since we met each other. Since he tutored me. Since we started hanging out at my apartment, theoretically to get Star to pay attention to him, but really, I just wanted him there to watch TV with and eat pizza with.

But I couldn't. I couldn't let those words out of my mouth because then I couldn't put them back. They would have been said, and there would be a clear delineation in the relationship between Gavin and me—*before* and *after.* Like BC and AD, it would be entirely different ways of telling time. And who knew what was waiting for me on the other side.

There was a risk. A risk that the other side carried that I wasn't willing to bare yet. A risk so great that it made me sick to my stomach thinking about it.

That he would just say goodbye. That he would leave and I would never speak to him again. That he would think it was all too much work, too much stress, and that dealing with me pining for him ruined his ability to spend any time with him at all.

I couldn't tell him that. Nor could I tell him that the very idea of spending the rest of my life never speaking to him felt like telling me I would never breathe again. I was as wrapped up as a person could be without actually dating someone. I needed him in my life. To be there, to listen to, to be listened to by, to stare at, and to laugh with. I needed Gavin's presence like I needed water to drink.

So I swallowed it. All of it. I swallowed it and tried to smile.

"Yeah," I lied. "I'm fine."

*Go big or go home. Lie like you mean it, Lila.*

"Are you sure?" he asked.

*Lie like a snake. Lie so hard that it becomes true.*

"Yeah. Just upset for you is all," I said.

He nodded slowly, and I wondered if he believed it. I wondered if he could see into my eyes and know the truth. Or if he took me at my word. My lying, good-for-nothing word.

I also didn't know which one I would prefer.

"I think, if it's all right with you, that I'd like to watch that show with you again."

"Sure," I said, turning away and pretending to fiddle with the bag my sandwich had come in. What I was really doing was brushing away the tears that had formed in the corner of my eye, threatening to spill down and wet me. Threatening to give away the whole game.

I crossed the room and tossed the bag into the trash can by the lamp in the corner. Then I ducked my head out past the curtain to take a look again outside. The guys were indeed gone. Or at least out of sight from here. But I wasn't worried about them crashing our room in the middle of the night. For as scared as Emma had been and cautious as Kevin had seemed, I believed Gavin.

They had no reason to come again. They thought the damage was done, that Gavin had no choice but to pay up. He was already pushed against the wall with a broken wing, knowing worse was ahead of him if he didn't follow their instructions.

I could breathe tonight.

I looked back up to Gavin, who had scooted himself onto one side of the bed, his hurt arm on the far side. He looked at me expectantly, motioning over to the other side of the bed. I felt my entire body seize up and my core warm like an oven. Gavin was asking me to get into bed with him.

"Aren't you uncomfortable in slacks?" I asked, a part of my mind dying to see if he would ask me to help him change out of them.

"Now that you mention it, yeah," he said. "Why don't you get comfortable and I'll go get ready for bed. You don't mind if I'm only in boxers, do you? I don't think Kevin's making it back down with any of my stuff."

"No, that's... that's just fine," I stuttered, hoping he didn't notice.

I crawled into the bed and glanced down, looking for any traces of blood or anything we might want to clean up first, but there was none. He had been careful not to bleed on anything. It was just another example of how surprisingly thoughtful he was. He had just taken a beating and was oozing plasma everywhere, but he had gone to extra lengths to not get any of it on my bed.

As he changed in the bathroom, I tossed off my shoes and debated changing into pajamas too. Finally, I hopped out of the bed, opened the drawer with the shorts, and quickly put a pair on. Yanking off my shirt, I reached for a T-shirt and heard the door of the bathroom opening.

Oh no.

I couldn't be caught in just my bra.

I spun around and pulled the shirt up over my head, realizing at the last moment that it wasn't a T-shirt at all. It was a tight tank top. It fell down over my head, and I yanked it over my chest as I heard him sit on the bed. How much had he seen? How much did he *want* to see?

I turned to him and somewhat disappointedly noticed he was looking at his phone. Maybe he hadn't noticed me at all.

He sat gingerly on the edge of the bed and tossed his socks down onto his shoes before spinning and lying back. I crossed the room to him and crawled in as well, both of us under the covers. Before I let myself get comfortable, I grabbed a pillow and put it between us, wrapping my arms around it and propping my head up by folding the other pillow in half.

"It was this one, right?" he asked, showing me his phone. He had it queued up to the episode that I last remembered watching before we fell asleep.

"Yup," I said.

"Awesome," he said, propping the phone on another pillow sitting on his bare stomach. I let my eyes languish on his chest and stomach for just a moment before forcing them onto the tiny screen.

We watched the show as he slowly relaxed. Eventually, the adrenaline and the insanity of the night wore off, and I heard him doze off, a light, adorable snore coming from his nose. I reached over and clicked the button to stop the show and picked up the phone, reaching over him to put it on the nightstand beside him.

It was there, with my arm stretched over him, that I realized I could just let gravity pull me down. I could let my arm stay over him, curled up beside him, listen to his heartbeat, and sleep myself. I knew already how comfortable it was to curl up with him and sleep. It would be glorious.

And then the morning would come.

Reluctantly, I pulled my arm back and, using the momentum, rolled right out of the bed. Gavin didn't move where he was. I pulled the blanket up over his chest and then went to the couch. Making a bed with the spare blanket there and dragging my pillow over, I curled up and tried not to cry as I exhaustedly fell asleep.

# Chapter Nineteen

## *Gavin*

I WOKE UP IN A SWEAT, the ghosts of a dream whispering through my brain like smoke, disappearing in the ether as I figured out where I was. I wasn't sure what the dream had been about, but it had been enough to make me sit up suddenly, sending shockwaves of pain over my shoulder and thumping inside my cheek under my eye.

Sitting in the soft light of the moonlight coming through the crack in the curtains over the window, I breathed deeply to try to regain my heartbeat's normal rhythm. A few moments later, I finally was able to simply breathe through my nose and felt calmer.

But awake.

I lay back down, trying to force my eyes closed, but it was no use. I was awake now. Wide awake. And nothing was going to put me back to sleep. Not for a bit, anyway.

Reluctantly, I rolled a bit and tried to get myself comfortable despite being on my hurt shoulder side. In the darkness of the room, I could see the mound on the couch that represented Lila. At some point, she had left the bed and gone over there to sleep. I couldn't blame her, I guess. I was the one who had slipped out in the middle of the night the last time we fell asleep together. She was returning the favor all around, it seemed.

I listened to her breathing softly from across the room and tried to let myself drift off to that, but it didn't work. I kept opening my eyes and staring at her. And the more I stared at her, the more I wanted to wake her up. Invite her over. Have her curl up in my arm and kiss the top of her head. Her lips. And more.

Standing up, sweeping my legs out of the bed and pushing them down into the soft carpet, I walked over to the window. It was desolate outside. The parking lot was quiet and empty of anything other than sleeping cars and the remnants of the fight. Someone was going to discover a broken mirror in the morning. I wondered if they had cameras over there. If they would see what happened.

I would find out, I guessed. No use worrying about it tonight.

The beach was also empty. Water lapped up over the sand and seemed soothing. I wanted to be down there, to let the water wash over my feet and see if the cooler air, the salt and sea would clear the thoughts that were racing over and over through my mind. Looking back at Lila, she seemed quite well asleep.

There was a problem, though. I didn't have a key. Not to her room, anyway. Thinking fast, I went to my slacks and pulled out one of my own room keys. I didn't bother putting on different clothes. It was still warm out there, according to my phone. Boxers looked as much like regular shorts as anything else, and there was no need to wear a shirt on a beach.

Propping the door open with the keycard for my own room so that it looked like it was shut, but a push could get me back inside, I slipped down the hall to the stairs and went down gingerly. I didn't really notice until I was going down them how much my legs and back hurt. The fight had taken a lot out of me, and I had been hit in various places. I was probably purple and bruised all over, enough that if anyone saw me out there without a shirt, they would have questions.

Thankfully, the lobby was empty, and when I went out of the door leading to the beach, no one was out there either. I walked quietly out to the edge of the water and let the water wash over my feet. It was cold, but not freezing. The hot weather was already warming it up, despite it only being spring. Apparently, Myrtle Beach hadn't had the same kind of surprisingly cold winter North Georgia had.

Still, it was cold enough that I didn't want to be perpetually pounded by the waves, so I sat back a little bit from the shoreline, where the water only occasionally reached me, and crossed my arms over my knees.

The stars glowed bright despite the city lights, and I listened to the sound of the lazy waves running along the sealine. In the distance, I could hear people farther down the beach, still enjoying their spring break. It was nearly five in the morning, but for some people, Spring Break meant being awake until the sun started a new day and drinking began again.

What was I going to do?

Out here, in the darkness, alone with the water, I felt myself clearly think for the first time in a while. The answers seemed to float up like foam on the water, leaving little trails of thought. Each one seemed so real, so perfect, and then it would dissolve into a new thought, with new trails.

I just had to choose.

For one, I was going to break up with Star.

I never should have pursued her in the first place, and I knew that now. I was enamored by a vision, an idea of what I wanted her to be, not who she was. Lila was right. Star was honest about who she was at all times. She didn't try to convince you she cared. You knew she didn't. But she was so alluring that you thought it might change. You convinced yourself of it.

But as I hurt myself over and over with her, I realized that I was wrong. She wasn't as alluring as I'd thought she was. What I knew about her now colored everything I thought I knew about her before. She wasn't the perfect creature who I thought she was when I helped her find her artwork in a swirling winter wind.

I was going to let her go, and she probably wouldn't even care. It would be surprising to her if it was hard for me. She never asked to be in a relationship. She just went along with whatever I said because she liked me. But the second I was out of the picture, she moved on. I probably didn't even need to break up with her. If I never contacted her again, I didn't know that she would even notice.

As for Lila...

I'd have to figure that out afterwards.

The big question, the one that was looming over me, was what I was going to do about the gang.

They had offered me a choice that first time in the parking lot. A choice that I told them then was impossible. A choice that they told me was my only two choices, and when they saw me at the club, they thought I didn't take them seriously. So they were going to force one of them.

They wanted me to throw the games I pitched in. They wanted me to throw beachball fastballs to the three-four guys and get hammered with homers. They wanted me to swing and miss on purpose when I came up to the plate. They wanted me to throw the games, so they could bet on them, and win. If they won ten thousand dollars on the bets, they would call it even, they said. They might even make it on the first two games, they said.

But then, if I refused...

If I refused, it was twenty thousand dollars, due Sunday. If I didn't have it, I wasn't going to make it to the championship game, assuming we qualified. Which, considering we were favorites, was a pretty good lock.

It was a dilemma. It would be so easy to throw the games, especially now. I could lie about my arm, then just go up there and throw BP fastballs until I got yanked. I was sure I'd get knocked around with the guys we were playing. They would take advantage quickly. I probably would only pitch for an inning before being yanked. One inning. Twice. And it would be over.

But then, if I did that, we wouldn't make it out of the Round Robin tournament to the finale. And I would have scouts see me look like a minor leaguer.

And worst, I would let my teammates down. I would let Coach down.

I would let Kevin down.

I couldn't do that. Not for them. Not for anyone. I couldn't throw a game.

So, twenty thousand dollars it was. That represented everything I had in the bank, but it would fix it. And then they would leave me and my friends alone. Hell, they would probably bet *on* me at that point. Everyone else was going to. No matter how dumb it would be with me being hurt like I was.

If I paid them off, it was going to be detrimental to my finances. I had been able to live off my scholarships and grants thus far without needing a job. It allowed me to focus solely on my academics and baseball. But now, that would change. I would have to find something to do for money. I might even have to move out of the place Kevin and I shared, because I wouldn't be able to pay the rent past June, when it was paid up until already.

Then again, I'd be free. Completely free. Because I would be damned if I had anything else to do with my father again. Mom was on the bubble, but Dad was done. I was done saving his ass. I was done using his last name. I was done with being his son. Prison or not, gangs or not, I was done with him for good. When I made the payment to the gang, I would let them know that I was done. That as far as I was concerned, I didn't give a shit if Dad owed them anything, they could do with him what they pleased.

I got the impression that if they couldn't leverage Dad's well-being against me, and my well-being certainly didn't matter to Dad, that they would probably leave me alone at that point. It would be nice to not ever have to worry about picking up the phone for them again. Never having to worry about saving their ass again. Or being guilted into running the store or coming home and paying for Christmas dinner again.

I would have to live off ramen for a while. Ramen and chicken breasts were an underrated combination. I could buy chicken in bulk, stick it in the freezer, buy a bottle of sriracha and ramen, and I'd be fine. It would suck after a while, but I could make it until the new school year. Then it should even out. And with no parents to worry about, I'd be okay. Major Leagues or not, I would be okay. I could land somewhere, doing something, even if I never made it to the bigs.

The sudden weight lifted off my shoulders at the idea that I didn't *have* to become a big-league player so I could take care of my parents was cathartic. I was starting to feel settled, like I might have a handle on everything. All it would cost me is my luxury for a few months. And my shoulder, I guessed. But that debt was already paid. Whatever happened afterward was up to me. I just had to gut through it or tell Coach I couldn't pitch. Either way, I would get through it.

Something moved behind me.

A chill ran down my spine as I envisioned the gang. I had no idea why they would be back. It wasn't like I could have gotten the money in the last few hours. Unless they were back solely for a fight and had waited outside of the hotel until four in the morning to do it, it didn't make sense for them to show up now.

I turned. Waiting to see that bald head behind me, my fist clenched. I didn't know if I was going to have to fight my way off the beach or not, but the shadow that was coming toward me, outlined by the streetlight behind it, wasn't bald, nor was it male.

Hair was tied high on the head, and the shadow reached up to take it down. Slowly, it moved into the moonlight and I could see who it was. It was Lila.

She was wearing extremely short shorts and a tight tank top. The stars shone above and behind her as she made her way toward me, looking like a siren. I stood, feeling a magnetic draw to her. Feeling like I had no choice. I needed to go to her.

Now.

Sand dug between my toes as I began to walk.

Toward her.

# Chapter Twenty

## *Lila*

WHEN I WOKE UP AND realized that yet again I was alone, my first thought was to be hurt by it. He did it again. He left in the middle of the night.

But as I sat up, I realized that this time couldn't be too much like the others. For one, his clothes were still here. And the door was still open, something stuck in the latch to keep it from closing all the way. The room didn't feel as empty as it felt pensive. Waiting. Like the room itself was holding its breath. He might not be in there, but that didn't mean he wasn't coming back.

Rubbing my eyes and cracking my neck, I tried to get my foot back to life by stomping it a few times. I had fallen to sleep in an awkward position on the couch, and my left foot had borne the worst of it. It fit my normal motif. I was so clumsy I could hurt myself sleeping.

Deciding not to let myself sink into the idea that he was disappearing like he had last time, I yawned and tried to decide what to do. I could wait, though with the lights out and the cracked window letting in the sound of the ocean, that was a recipe for falling asleep again. I could see if he went back to his own room, which would make sense, since he was without most of his other stuff.

Or I could do what I was almost positive he had done. Go down to the beach to think.

As a matter of fact, when I stood, I peeked out of the window and saw a shape on the sand, just by the water, that looked an awful lot like Gavin. Whoever it was, they were sitting out there shirtless.

A fast-moving and electric feeling ran up my spine, and I shuddered.

The heat from outside was in constant combat with the air conditioner, so I went ahead and closed the window, moving to the mirror above the dresser and looking at my reflection.

I was about to do something that was potentially very stupid.

And I was thrilled.

I brushed my hair back into a ponytail and grabbed my room key cards. I was going to go out there and give him one of them, if he wanted it. And either we were going to come back to the room together, he was going to take the room key and go to his room to gather things, or I was going to be very sad when I got back. But either way, the room didn't need to be propped open anymore. I let it shut with a click as I walked out into the hallway and down to the stairwell.

Before I got to the door leading out of the main floor to the beach, I looked around to see if anyone was up and watching. Aside from the clerk at checkout, who was highly engrossed in his phone at the moment, no one was around. Part of me didn't care if they had been. At this point, if people thought something... well... let them think.

I was just going to talk to him. If people got the wrong idea, then it would all be cleared up soon enough. Or if they got the right idea... well, that would be cleared up too.

But the thing was, Gavin had had a really tough night. As much as my own inner turmoil suggested that maybe now was the time to profess that my feelings had gone way past being his wingman, the truth was, it wasn't likely the time or place. Star wasn't around and couldn't defend herself. Gavin had literally been beaten up defending himself and me from three men. He had bruises and cuts, and his shoulder was a mess. He was dealing with the possibility that his entire career might be in jeopardy because his parents were apparently lowlifes.

Now wasn't the time for me and him to hash out what all the longing looks, the close dancing, and the almost kiss were about.

Unless he wanted to talk about it.

I *was* bringing him a key to my room. One that I wanted him to keep. It implied that I wasn't just making sure he got back in tonight safely, but that I was willing to have him in my room whenever he wanted.

For whatever reason he wanted.

I could rationalize it away, lie to myself about how I was just looking out for his well-being and safety. I could try to make it seem more like I was just being a really good friend. But I knew the truth, deep down. If he was really done with Star, and I thought he was, then I didn't want to take the chance on him not knowing exactly how I felt about him.

Crossing the sand, I had no doubt that the figure by the water was Gavin. I could not only see the easily recognizable frame outlined against the moonlight reflecting off the water, but the cut that ran across his shoulder and back that was still healing. It shone in the light. Something that would likely remind him of tonight for weeks to come as it healed. Whether he wanted to remember it or not.

The sand was still warm on my toes as I neared him. The night was still hot and stuffy, but there were no clouds above us. No threat of rain. Just a rolling ocean and above it, a black, starry sky. A white, bright moon hung high as well, and as I glanced up, a star fell. I felt myself hold my breath in as I frantically made a wish.

Gavin turned his head, noticing me as I got closer, and I stopped. My heart was thumping so loudly in my chest I was sure he could hear it over the roar of the ocean. He was gazing at me through a swollen eye and a bruised body that still was as attractive as it always had been. I found myself wanting to kiss his bruises, to soothe them.

To hold him.

He stood, and my heart went from thumping in my chest to hammering in my throat. I couldn't swallow. The salty sea breeze blew errant strands of hair across my face as I stuttered for some semblance of control. It was like I was pulled toward him, almost as if there were giant magnets in our chests.

The smoldering, deep stare coming from his eyes locked on to mine, and I felt frozen in the heat. I could no more move a muscle voluntarily than I could have lifted a car. Yet I was still walking. Still closing the gap between us. And I was getting faster.

We were almost running when we got within feet of each other and slowed down. But not stopped.

Our bodies met each other in the sand, and I felt like I couldn't breathe. My eyes were focused solely on his and his on mine. Slowly, he closed the last little bit of space between us, and our bodies brushed against each other. I could feel the hard, sculpted chest against my breasts, and the heart pumping beneath was slamming against my ribcage like a jackhammer.

His breath fell on mine, and while mine was coming out in stuttering whisps, his was low and slow. Calm. Collected. In control. However long I had thought about a moment like this, it was as if he had thought more. He was prepared. Or at least unconcerned, and not in a nonchalant way. But in the way of someone who knows what is about to happen.

And is *completely okay with it.*

"I..." I began, looking into his face, a mask of emotion and pain and swelling. The words fell away like loose sand under our feet, washing into the ocean.

A wave crashed below, several feet away, and a rush of water ran up over our toes. It was cold and bracing, and it should have snapped me out of any trance I was in, any spell that had me thinking abnormally.

But there was no breaking this moment. There was no changing the future. What was going to happen was going to happen regardless of if Mother Earth tried to swallow us whole right then and there. If an earthquake broke out between us, I had no doubt he would hold the world together in his hands until our moment had climaxed.

Until...

"I..." I tried again.

Gavin lifted his hand and placed one finger on my lips. Gently touching them, depressing them with the weight of his skin. I felt like taking it into my mouth, just to taste him. But my mind was locked, unable to think or do. Just the knowledge that a part of him was pressing against my lips was enough to weaken my knees and end the thousand different thoughts in my mind and replace them with a million new ones. Thoughts about if anything else would touch my lips and when and how, and for how long?

Slowly, he reached down with his other hand and stuffed it into his pocket. I forced myself to break his eye contact and look away from its commanding, intoxicating gaze. The world swirled with my eyes, like I was drunk. Colors mixed together, and motion seemed to blur. It was like I had stared at a light for too long and then looked at something dark. Perhaps I had.

He struggled for a second to pull whatever he was getting out, and I realized it was his phone as he nearly dropped it. Catching it, he brought it up to show me the home screen. Then he hit a button and pulled something up. When he turned the phone again, my throat caught. It was the message thread with Star.

He smirked, and I felt like my body might melt there on the sand. He pulled the phone back to him and began typing, stopping for a moment and looking away as he seemed to be looking for the right words. Then he finished and breathed deeply through his nose. My fingers tingled, and my head felt light. I realized I hadn't let out a breath or taken one in for a while.

I wanted to speak, to say something. Panic was running through my body and making my mind go a million directions at once. I felt like I was standing on the edge of a cliff, teetering over and looking down into a sea of clouds. What was below them I didn't know. It could be jagged rocks of heartache and sorrow. Or the warm, thick pool of hope and decadence.

Part of me wanted him to stop. To wait. To talk before he said anything to her. What would I do if he said what I thought he would say? How would she take it? Our friendship would be ruined.

But another part of me, a part of me that longed to not be the big girl who shook the plates in the cabinet and looked like someone had edited a giant into photos of Star and me together, that part of me didn't. That part of me was screaming that this was the man of my dreams. Of anyone's dreams. And that Star didn't want him. She didn't want anyone or anything. She was Star. She took life as it came, and this was just another blip. But that I deserved happiness. I deserved to have what I wanted, regardless of if Star wanted it too.

It might nuke our relationship. She might throw me out, and I would have to find somewhere else to live. Our wonderful apartment would belong to her, and her rich father would pay for it. I would probably end up on the other side of campus in the tiny places.

Near Gavin.

It wouldn't be so bad, really. To be on my own. Not that I would be alone.

The fear and the hope and the wonder of if any of that would actually happen were warring in my brain. It was just as likely that Star would shrug at any news of Gavin and me and move on like nothing had changed. Because to her, nothing ever did. All that mattered to Star was what Star did. What Star wanted. And if she didn't want Gavin, then she wouldn't care.

But I cared. And Gavin cared. And as he hit the send button on his message, his eyes floated back to mine, and I could see that while all that care was still there, it had changed. No longer did he care because he wanted her. Because he lusted for her or crushed on her or whatever feelings he once had for her. But because he had empathy.

He didn't want to hurt her.

But with that message, a message that he was turning the phone so I could see, he was telling her that if it was a choice between her happiness and his own, he was going to choose himself.

He was going to choose me.

The screen was too bright in the darkness, and it kind of hurt my eyes to look. I read it and re-read it, not really comprehending it at first. My brain just didn't want to process it because it didn't feel real. It couldn't actually be true.

Nothing that good ever happened to me.

"I think we should see other people," the message read.

His finger was still pressed against my lip, though lightly. It was barely there, pushing the gentlest touch against me. But as he pulled the phone back and stuffed it in his pocket, he let go. I rocked gently, almost moving toward him just to feel his touch again.

But he didn't let me fall. He was right there, his strong body, so beaten from the fight and yet still so resilient, held me up. And as I parted my lips, his own dipped down toward them.

This time there was no one to bump into us.

This time there was no one to stop us.

This time, I sank into the moment, touching my lips to his and feeling more powerful than the sea as it crashed another wave and sent another pool of cold water over our feet. It was like it was waking me up to a new reality.

I kissed him back.

# Chapter Twenty-One

## *Gavin*

THERE WAS NO STOPPING now.

Our lips had touched, finally, and the need for her only grew. Not satisfied with the taste of her lips or the feel of her skin on mine, the tenderness of her touch combined with the roaring passion that lay just beneath, I felt an urge unlike anything I had ever felt. To kiss her harder, to feel her deeper, to entwine my body with hers more completely than either of us had ever known.

Her lips were soft and sweet. I wanted to touch them forever. Simply holding myself back when my finger touched them was hard enough, but it was worth it. The decision had been made, and in an instant, I knew what to do. Star had been informed. It was over. Whatever it was to begin with. It certainly wasn't a normal relationship.

I pulled her tight to my body, relishing in the thin fabric of her clothes against the very little of my own. No matter how much my bruises hurt, none of it mattered now. I felt like a Greek god. I could do anything.

We sank into each other and then down into the sand. Disappearing over the edge of the dune to an empty, secluded world of our own, our kiss became more passionate. As our bodies hit the sand, I lay back and pulled her on top of me. It was weird for me to not want to press over top of her, but I wanted to be smothered by her. I wanted her all over me, in a way that I had never felt before. I wanted to be all-encompassed by her. Until all I could feel on my body was sand and her skin. Her lips. Her breath.

Her hands were pressed into my chest, but she wasn't pushing. She was touching. Her fingers trailed down over my chest and to my stomach as my own rolled over her back. Her breasts were pressed into my stomach, and my cock hardened at the warmth of her core over it. My hands slid down to her ass, going inside her shorts and squeezing her soft, bare skin. Pulling her hard down onto me.

She moaned in my ear. A moan that was breathy and heavy with passion. She could feel my hardness under her, burying into her and only blocked by two layers of soft, stretchy fabric. The ridge of my cock slid between the folds of her pussy, and she gasped. But her hips moved expertly over me. She rode me, my cock surely brushing against her clit.

One hand slid around to her waist and climbed. Up under her loose shirt, I felt the swell of her breast against my thumb as my other hand moved to my shorts. I wanted to pull them down, to let her feel me at my hardest, without something between us. My thumb hooked under the waistband, and I began to pull down. The curly, soft hair of my center brushed against her stomach.

Suddenly, she pushed up, causing breath to escape me and pain to shoot up my shoulder. She pulled away, shuffling on knees in deep sand until she could get to her feet. She backed up, eyes burning into mine with a mixture of confusion and desire. Eyes that told me she wanted to strip down right then and have me inside her, but she couldn't. She wouldn't.

A crash of water behind her sent bubbling, rushing, cold sea over her feet and up to my own. She stood out against the moonlight and stars, a goddess to me, her shirt twisted and showing more of her stomach than I had ever seen and a slight hint of the underside of one breast. It was enough that my cock pressed harder against my shorts, and I internally begged her to come back.

But she stood, silently, eyes bouncing between mine as she ran her hands through her hair and then looked away. When she looked back, the passion had been replaced by pain. My heart sunk.

"I can't…" she said hoarsely, her voice barely above the sound of a whisper against the crashing waves behind her. "I can't."

"Why?" I said, sitting up on my elbows. I didn't want to go to her. Not yet. It would seem too domineering, too aggressive. She would run, like a deer into the woods, and I needed to be careful. Slow and quiet.

"I just can't," she said, then seemed to rally. It was almost like she had been searching for a reason, like she knew one existed but had been ignoring and now had found it again. "Star. She hasn't read that message. As far as she's concerned, you two are still together."

"Okay," I said, shaking my head a little.

"And even when she does," she said. "I … I can't. She's my friend. My best friend. And my roommate. I can't just date her ex. Especially before she even knows that he's her ex. I just can't."

"Lila, wait," I said, sitting up.

"No," she said firmly, and I knew the moment was over. It was lost. That was as close as I was going to come to filling my cup with Lila and living in the bliss of that sensation.

"No?"

"No," she said again. "I have to go. Now. I think you should go back to your own room. I will give Emma your stuff tomorrow to give Kevin."

"Lila, just wait," I began.

"No," she said. "I can't. I just can't. I'm sorry, Gavin. I just can't."

She walked away, stomping more accurately as she tried to get through the ever-wetting sand. I didn't try to stop her. There was no use. She was gone.

Frustrated, hurt, and angry, I threw myself back onto the sand.

What happened? What had brought that thought into her mind? Did I move too fast? Was it the act of touching her that brought it on? Was it all too real? Too passionate? Was she worried she would go further than she wanted?

I could empathize with that. I wanted her, more than I had ever wanted anyone before. More than I had wanted Star by an order of magnitude. But if she wasn't ready, if she needed to move slower than that, I could understand. I could deal. Hell, I had dealt with Star taking things at a glacier-pace, and as I thought about it, I didn't actually like her nearly as much as I did Lila. I just liked the idea of her. The glamour of her. Star was like a fairy, and her image was enough to blind you to the fact that what was projecting it was shallow and empty. A shell.

But Lila... Lila was real. She was funny and sweet and smart. And sexy. She moved with a grace I was positive she had no idea she had. She cut through reality like a sword, slicing a shape for herself in it. At least that's how I saw her. It's how I had always seen her.

I was just too stupid to admit it to myself because of my shallow, silly crush on Star.

And now, as Lila stomped away, I realized I had done this all to myself. What came over me in the first place? What was going on in my brain?

Lila and Star were close, at least as close as Star was to anyone. Lila protected Star in a lot of ways, caring for her and absolving her of all the tiny little sins she committed by simply being her. Star was always saying or doing something that could be hurtful to those around her, but Lila never let it get to her. Never let her know. And always tried to foster a sense of peace and calm so Star could create. So she could be uniquely, authentically herself.

The only time she ever meddled in that was to help me get near her. Lila helped me get close, and why? Because I helped her with her studies? Sure, that might have been it at first. But after a few times of hanging out, was that really what was going on anymore? Was I even really coming over for anything other than hanging out with Lila?

In my mind, I was waiting to get laid. I was waiting until Star put down her defenses and I got my hands on her body and let myself find out if it was everything I had built it up to be. And I knew, deep down, I knew it wouldn't be. Being with Star would have been a sham. A joyless mark on a bedpost. A name to add to the list. A conquest that I would have made.

But it wouldn't mean anything.

But Lila...

In just those seconds, those few seconds our lips had pressed together, I felt the earth move. More than just sand slipping away into the current, I felt fault lines crack and the sky part and the light of the universe fill me up. My bruises and cuts didn't matter. Not even down in the dirt. I could handle the pain. I could handle the annoyance.

If it meant one more second of touching her. Of holding her. Of kissing her.

Of loving her.

I winced at the thought. That word... I had never felt that before. I had never even thought it in relation to a girl. I loved my parents, though they tortured me. I loved Kevin as my best friend. I loved baseball. But I had never loved a girl.

I hadn't even dated Lila, and yet...

Our kiss had been our first, and yet...

Our bodies had never crushed into each other, our nakedness eliminating any pretention, any apprehensiveness, and yet...

And yet...

I put my palms over my eyes and lay there, my hardened body softening and exhaustion starting to take over. I had left my key in her door, blocking the latch. I needed to go get it. One last insult to the injury.

I sat up, brushing as much sand off me as I could, and turned toward the hotel. My leg was suddenly heavy, a numbness in the thigh that had temporarily disappeared returning and in spades. I felt tired. Tired in my bones.

Trudging up the small dune to where the sand leveled out, I nearly fell once. What was I going to do tomorrow? I was in piss-poor shape to play, but I had to. I wasn't going to let the team down.

Once back in the hotel, I was keenly aware of how little clothing I was wearing at two in the morning. With just my shorts on, covered in sand, I looked like I had been doing something lascivious out there. I almost had. Either way, the guy at the desk gave me a somewhat knowing nod and grin. I felt my stomach turn.

Rather than go up the stairs, I went to the elevator, watching as the grin turned to a frown as the night clerk fetched a broom and dustpan as the doors shut. He was going to have to sweep up after me because I was shedding so much onto the floor. I wanted to feel bad for him, but I just couldn't muster up any more pity for anyone that wasn't myself.

I stopped on the girls' floor, making my way toward Lila's door. It was shut now, completely, and I almost knocked. But it wouldn't do any good. Even if I had, she wouldn't answer. And even if by some miracle, she did answer, it wouldn't change anything. She couldn't do this. Not until Star knew. Not until Star said something. And maybe not even then.

Glancing down, I saw my keycard, sitting on the ancient carpet that looked like it was out of a 1990s nostalgia picture. Ocean blue with weird triangular shapes in yellow, red, and green, it almost camouflaged the red keycard. As I bent to pick it up, my back protested with a series of pops and cracks.

Shuffling back to the elevator, I made it before it moved back down and was able to walk right back on. Apparently, the night clerk hadn't been in a hurry to clean the elevator out. Just to let me know he had to. I guess that was the order of the day. People telling me what I should feel. I should feel responsibility for my parents. I should feel pain. I should feel guilt over Star and my feelings for Lila. I should feel shame for making the clerk sweep.

All I really felt at that moment was tired.

When the elevator stopped at my floor, I got out, noticing that Kevin's room was dark. Good for him, at least. I hoped he enjoyed himself. Emma certainly looked like she was going to.

I opened the door to my room before I remembered the reason I had been staying at Lila's. The off chance that something could go wrong. That they might be waiting for me. But as the door swung open, the lights still on from where I left them earlier, I saw that no one was waiting for me. No one was there at all.

The door beside me cracked open, and I saw Kevin's face pop out. He saw me, looked back into his room for a second, and then slipped his massive body out, keeping one foot inside.

"Hey, bud," he said. "Coming to get supplies?"

"No, I'm staying here tonight," I said. "You're off duty."

"You sure, boss?"

"I'm sure," I said. "Good night, Kev."

"Night, Gav," he said.

I closed the door behind me and went to the bathroom, starting up a shower. At least I could be clean before I slept. Though I'd rather be covered in sand. And Lila.

# Chapter Twenty-Two

## *Lila*

I BARELY MADE IT TO my room before I collapsed into a shield of tears against the reality of outside of the cocoon and remainder of the dream of his presence. It still smelled like him. I hated it. Remnants of him were everywhere. The dice on the counter. His clothes piled by the bed. A bloodstain on the sheet. Hell, the first thing to greet me was his room key, which I let fall onto the carpet as I walked inside.

It had taken everything I had to make it into the room at all. I slammed the door to the stairwell open, unpleasantly surprised that the adrenaline and strength that had propelled me since I ran into him downstairs and decided to join him on a night out was gone. Now I felt like I was going to fall down right there on the steps, somewhere between the first and second floors.

Pushing myself, I held on to the railing on both sides and willed myself to my room. The feeling of panic, of impending badness that I only ever felt rushing to the bathroom with a stomach prepared to return anything I had eaten and drank back to the world, had filled me until I was in my room. But rather than throw up, it was a deep, guttural growl of pain. Of tears that had been threatening to burst like a dam while standing on that beach that cascaded down my cheeks in a mad rush for my chin.

I collapsed onto the floor by the dresser, heaving in my cries. Months of built-up emotion, tension, longing, and guilt had come to a head. It had overflowed in a kiss so pure, so filled with passion and desire that it felt like a lightning rod being stuck from the top of my head to the tips of my toes. He had brought me down into the sand with him as our hands roamed over each other's bodies, and he'd touched me in ways I had only fantasized. I could *feel* how much he wanted me as he pressed his cock into my core, and I'd reacted by rocking my body over him.

I had been desperate. I had been clamoring.

I had been wrong.

I couldn't do it. Not until I knew for sure Star was done with him, and even then... What was I going to do? How had I gotten myself into this mess? And surely, it was my mess. My mess at not being good enough at my studies that I needed Gavin as a tutor. My mess at agreeing to be his wingman with my roommate if he helped me pass. My mess at watching them grow into a proto-couple all while I harbored desire for him. My mess at getting sick and having him take care of me. My mess at going with him to the club and relishing in his attention, in his body being pressed into mine.

My mess for going down to the beach. My mess for kissing him back.

My mess.

I was suddenly so very tired. I crawled, tears streaming down my face, to the edge of the bed and grabbed a handful of sheets and blankets. I yanked, not wanting to smell him as I drifted off to sleep and yet at the same time, wishing more than anything he would just come to the door. To knock. I was weak, and I would let him in.

I would let him in, in every way.

As I tore at the bed, the tears began to subside, drying up out of sheer exhaustion. I didn't have the strength to cry anymore. Instead, when the sheets were off the bed, I used everything I had left to get up to my feet. I brought an extra sheet and blanket with me everywhere I went in my suitcase. It was a tick of mine. I hated using the sheets that a hotel had on the bed when I first got there. I often replaced them my-self.

Now I had sheets lying in my suitcase from my first night. I had washed them myself. With every last bit of my energy, I grabbed the sheet and the blanket, throwing the sheet onto the bed and wrapping myself in the blanket before falling into the bed. I didn't want to use the pillows because they might remind me of him, so I just bundled part of the blanket under my temple and closed my eyes.

For a brief moment, I thought to myself that I would never get to sleep. That the night had been too much, and that I would be thinking about those moments in the sand until the sun rose.

Then I fell into a deep, fitful, almost instant sleep. Like my brain took pity on my heart and simply shut off the lights.

MY ALARM HAD THANKFULLY been set to go off every day at the same time. The same with a backup alarm a half hour later. And a third, more insistent alarm with a sound that I absolutely hated third, ten minutes after that.

Otherwise, I would have slept for a lot longer.

Groggily, I turned off the third alarm, forcing myself to sit up so I didn't just shut my eyes and go back to sleep again. The memories of the night before had not faded. They were as prevalent as they had been when I fell asleep. So was the decision that I knew had to be made. It bore down on me with an insistence that was impossible to ignore.

I couldn't just start dating Gavin. If he was even still interested after how I left him.

Not until Star knew what happened. And that meant everything. She needed to know how I had been having feelings for him for months. How I had helped set them up. How I had gone down to the beach knowing that it might end up with something happening, and that when it did, I didn't fight it until it had almost gone too far.

I needed to let her know that I understood if she didn't want to ever hear from me again. That all she would have to do is tell me that I needed to move out and that I would figure out a way to do it. But that she needed to also know that if she was against us being together because she still had feelings for Gavin, that my suspicions about her activities and the way she felt was wrong and she was head over heels for him... that I would back off.

I was the bad guy. I knew it. I was attempting to steal her boyfriend away. I needed to accept that. And accept that I wasn't just going to get what I wanted.

Star deserved to know what happened as early as possible. So pulling my phone to me as I stood up, blearily making my way to the bathroom to wash off day-old makeup and start a shower, I opened a notepad app and started composing my message.

I didn't send it, not yet, not until I got out of the shower and was thinking as clearly as I could. I needed to make sure I said everything I needed to say, just in case it was the last time she ever spoke to me. It needed to be brutally honest, but also let her know how much she meant to me. How much this tore me up too.

The water got hot quickly, and I stripped down and stepped inside without bothering to go get clothes for later. I had to put on my uniform when I got out. I had a game to play. No matter how shitty I felt, I had batters to strike out.

I stayed in the shower as long as I could, letting the water relax my muscles and the steam clear my mind. By the time I was clean, I also felt like I could think again. I opened the curtain and stepped out into the bathroom, and my eyes fell on the pile of clothes by the bed.

Instantly, a flash of the night before hit me. His body pressed against mine. His hand had pushed his shorts down enough that the soft, curly hair at his core touched my skin, and I had gotten an idea of how thick, long, and wide his cock was. I could nearly feel it inside of me as it brushed through my folds, only separated by the soft cloth of our shorts.

Instinctively, my fingers slid to my clit, and my other hand fell across my right breast. I wanted to sink into the memory. I wanted to relieve some of the tension that had been built up and not released. I wanted to think about what he would have done had I not stopped him. Had I not stopped myself.

I wanted to think about him being inside me. Of his lips on my skin. Of the climax I could have had, out there in the open on the beach, completely disregarding whoever might have seen.

No.

I stopped myself, shoving my hands down by my sides and stomping into the main room, dripping wet. I marched to the dresser and yanked open the one that had my collection of sports bras and panties. I threw them on quickly, so as to not let myself be tempted any more, and then dug for my uniform in the stack of clean clothes by my suitcase.

By the time I had the pants and shirt on, I felt a little better. I still had other pieces to put on, other things to do to get ready, but there were a few things to take care of first. Namely, I gathered up the sheets in a bundle and tossed them out of the door. Housekeeping would pick them up and leave new ones. I didn't want them inside the room, so I stuck the Do Not Disturb hanger on the knob.

Then I took Gavin's clothes, touching them with just my fingertips, and shoved them in a plastic bag. If Emma and Kevin were going to be an item beyond last night, I would give them to her to give to Gavin. I didn't plan on talking to him until I had spoken to Star.

Maybe for a few days after.

I pulled open the phone and read through the note I had made. Deciding there was nothing more to add, I copied it and then opened a text box for Star. Pasting it inside, I hit send and then turned the phone off. I didn't want to see any other messages. Any other reminders of life beyond softball. I needed the focus. I needed the distraction from life and to remind myself that the only way I was going to graduate was if I kept my scholarship. And that meant striking motherfuckers out.

I would deal with the fallout, and there would most certainly be fallout, when I got back after the game.

It was a super long text. Longer than was allowed, it turned out. It had to be split into two. But I was satisfied I had covered everything. I talked about how I had helped set Gavin up with her. About how I'd felt something for him as far back as Thanksgiving. About how I pushed those thoughts away because she was starting to notice him and he was adamant about her.

I told her about the long nights when we got here, and how frustrated we both were at her not being communicative. How it seemed like she wasn't taking the relationship seriously and how Gavin mentioned he didn't think it was working out. How hurt he was when she didn't care he'd gotten beat up.

But then, I told her that I was still at fault. That I bore the responsibility of being the person that went down to the beach. I bore the responsibility of kissing him back. I bore the responsibility of falling into the sand with him, of going too far, and that when I pulled back, the damage had been done. That I had crossed a line and that as her best friend, I should have known better.

I told her that I would always be there for her. But I understood if that wasn't what she wanted.

Then I told her I was shutting off my phone to go concentrate on softball. That I would read any messages she sent me later. That if nothing else, we could talk when she got home from France.

And that I missed her.

It was true. I did miss her. I had intended on her being here with me during the whole trip. Even if I had resented the idea that she would be sharing a room, and a bed, with Gavin, I was excited to have her with me at the beach. I had envisioned evenings of us going out together to dance and drink. Of us swimming in the ocean, even if I would be jealous of her ever-ready bikini body. Of stealing her for at least one night of girl's sleepover.

But all that was on hold and probably over for good.

Deciding not to even bring the phone with me just in case I was tempted to check my messages, I stuffed it on the charger and finished getting dressed. Then I grabbed my bat bag and my room key and headed out of the door.

I didn't want to run into Gavin, who likely had early morning practice as well, so I slipped down the stairwell and through the gym to the other side of the hotel. From there, I followed the path to the fields and was thankful again for them being right next to the hotel. I could see everything that was going on. Including who was coming and when.

Hours before everyone else joined, I was down on the field, stretching, throwing against the cage, doing what I could to get myself focused. Then, when they all filtered in, I grabbed Saraya, one of our catchers, and started warming up. By the time evening fell and the lights came on, I had been practicing pretty much all morning and day, with only a small stop to eat when Emma brought me lunch.

I was limber. I was warm. I was focused.

And I turned every single bit of frustration I had into fire in the game. Those poor girls never knew what hit them.

# Chapter Twenty-Three

## *Gavin*

I WOKE UP EARLY, KNOWING the day was going to suck the second I opened my eyes.

Pain was everywhere. My arms, my legs, my face. My back and hips. Even my eyes hurt.

I struggled to find the phone under my pillow and shut off the alarm. I wanted to go back to sleep, to see if I could will the pain and grogginess away. But I couldn't. Not after last night. Not after *everything*.

I had two notifications on my phone besides the alarm. Messages from Mom and Star. I sighed. I wasn't ready to read Star's yet. Not for a while, I figured. I just didn't have it in me for her to tell me what a horrible person I was. And for her to be justified in it.

Opening Mom's message, I blinked as I tried to get my eyes to focus. The swelling had seemed to go down a little over my eye, but it was still pushing down a bit. It was going to be a hell of a thing to convince Coach I was fine. It was going to be another whole hell of a thing to actually seem fine when game time came. If I pulled it off, I should probably start taking classes in the theater department.

Mom's message was simply a question mark. Ever the caring and eloquent woman, Mom had only needed one character to express her feelings. She wanted to know what happened, but I knew that telling her about me being jumped wasn't it. She didn't care about that. Not in the grand scheme of things. She just wanted to know if *she* was going to be safe. If I was going to handle the situation and save her ass again. Like I had done so many times before.

Closing her message, I opened my bank app and checked my balance in savings. I had just enough. After I pulled it out, I would have roughly two hundred dollars to live on. Thankfully, I had paid my rent for the semester already. Ramen was going to be my friend for a while.

Checking for local branches, I found there was one just a block away from the hotel. I wouldn't even need to get a ride. It was within walking distance. At least something was going right for me. Of course, that meant walking the block over there, and at the moment I felt like every bone in my body might just go on strike if I tried, but it was better than finding a ride. That would require money that now I didn't have.

I opened Mom's message again and typed out a response.

"I'm taking care of it."

I didn't expect a response, not this early in the morning. Mom was notorious for going to bed at four and waking up somewhere around three in the afternoon. It had been one of the reasons I got very good at making my own breakfasts and sending myself off to school in the morning at a very young age. Mom certainly wasn't going to be able to do it very often.

Surprisingly, I got one back immediately. It was a series of emojis. Smiley faces and kissy faces and red hearts. I didn't have the heart or the energy to tell her what this cost. To tell her that, in effect, this was the last I wanted to hear from her for a long time. If ever. And certainly the last I would ever want to hear from my father.

That would have to wait. It was going to be a conversation I might want to have in person. At the home that I planned on grabbing everything I wanted out of and never going to again. Assuming Mom hadn't already burned it down for insurance money.

I shoved the phone back in my pocket, still keenly aware of Star's unread message waiting in my inbox. Then I got up and gingerly went through my suitcase. Finding a pair of jeans and a baseball-cut T-shirt, I slipped those on and transferred the phone and wallet to it. They would cover up most of the bruises. My hat would help cover up my face too. At least somewhat.

Shoving my sneakers on, I slipped out of the door, waiting for a moment to see if I heard Kevin coming to his door to see me. I didn't, but what I did hear was some very distinctly feminine giggling. For the first time since last night, I felt the hint of a grin.

Good for Kevin.

I went down into the lobby and grabbed a toiletries bag from the front desk before heading out. It was imperfect, but it would be at least something I could keep the cash in. I didn't think anyone would find it too suspicious if I was carrying a bag from the hotel. At least I didn't think they would think there was twenty thousand dollars in it.

The walk to the bank wasn't as excruciating as I thought it would be. The orange juice that I'd grabbed along with the bag helped wake me up some and getting my muscles moving warmed them up enough to not scream in pain the whole time. As I walked into the bank, I was keenly aware of the stares from the other customers and the clerks. I looked like hell.

"How can I help you?" a perky and cheerful middle-aged woman asked as I made my way to the counter. She had the look of someone who was trying very hard not to hit the panic button under the desk.

"Hi, I need to make a fairly major withdrawal," I said, knowing her fingers were inching closer to the button just on that sentence alone. "I have an account. Here's my ID."

"Sure thing," she said in a voice way too high to be normal. She took my ID and disappeared behind the counter, moving to a computer on the other side and conversing with a woman in a smart business suit. Both of them joined me at the counter when she was done doing whatever it was she was doing with my ID.

"Mr. Freeman?" the woman in the suit asked. "Hi, I'm Tamara, the bank manager here. Sue tells me you want to make a major withdrawal."

"Yes," I said. "Do you have an office? I would rather talk about it in private."

"Sure," she said. "Right this way."

Walking through a pair of saloon style doors, the bank manager went to a small office, and I followed her. When I sat down in the leather chair across from her desk, she shut the door and clicked the lock. Part of me wondered if she had triggered some kind of lock that would keep me in if I decided to go ballistic with a gun or something. She was acting awfully funny.

"So what can I help you with?" she said, typing something into her computer.

"I have a savings account. Last four digits 4631. I need to withdraw twenty-thousand dollars from it in cash."

"Oh, my," she said. "That *is* a major one. May I ask what it's for?"

"No."

There was silence for a moment as she did a double take and then a long look at me. Then she folded her hands on the desk and leaned over it toward me.

"Mr. Freeman, clearly, this money is yours. You can do with it whatever you like. But we here at First Bank of the Union, we care more about our customers than their portfolio. This would mark a very unusual transaction for any account, but especially for yours."

"I know," I said.

She turned back to her computer and moved the mouse for a moment before scrolling through something.

"It looks like here that this was from a scholarship? In Georgia? What are you doing here in South Carolina, Mr. Freeman?"

"Playing baseball," I said. "I am in a tournament down the street."

"Oh, the college tournament," she said, brightening up. "Of course. I knew that was going on this week. So you are playing in that tournament?"

"Yes. Can I have my money please?"

She seemed frustrated and sighed.

"Mr. Freeman, if there is a financial emergency, there are other options than simply liquidating your account. We have a multitude of small personal loans that I am sure could help with whatever purchase you are looking to make..."

"I don't want to take a loan," I said. "I want to withdraw my money. I have decided to do something other than keep it in a savings account. I don't really wish to talk about it any further."

There was another awkward silence.

"Mr. Freeman, may I ask you one more question?"

Now it was my turn to sigh.

"Sure."

"Are you in any trouble? I notice that you seem to have some fresh bruises on your face. If this is something that involves illegal activity, I am bound to alert the authorities as part of my job as a bank manager."

I pulled the hat up and stared at her through what I could see in the reflection of the window behind her was a pretty dark shiner.

"Tamara?" I asked. "I got into a fight last night. I was dancing with a girl, and a fight broke out and a guy punched me in the face. That's why I have a black eye and this scratch. It has nothing to do with the withdrawal that I have been planning on for a few days. I want to spend the money on a car and some baseball equipment. A pitch clock, to be precise. And some one-on-one time with a legendary pitcher who is offering a class next week. It is a series of purchases, not just one, and I need cash to make them happen. Now will you please let me have my money?"

I hated lying to her, but it was better than the alternative. And it seemed to work. Her mouth, which had dropped a bit when she saw my eye, had snapped shut. She turned back to her computer, typing a few things and then turning back to me, put her hands on the table to stand.

"You can stay right here, Mr. Freeman. I will be right back with your cash. Is there any specific way you would like it?"

"Hundreds are fine," I said.

She nodded curtly and stood, unlocking the door and leaving it cracked open as she left. I wondered what the conversation between her and Sue was going to be like.

When she returned, she had a fabric envelope with several stacks inside it. She set them down on the table and pulled them out, lining them up one by one and counting them out.

"Now this is twenty thousand in hundreds. I can open each one and count them for you if you would like."

"No, I trust you," I said. "Thank you."

"Thank you," she said. "I hope that you continue to do business here. I see you still have a balance in your savings of two hundred and four dollars, along with a checking account balance of thirty-six dollars."

"I'm sure I will," I said, standing. "Do you mind if I have this envelope?"

"Sure," she said. "Normally I can't, but we just got a shipment of replacements. Just be careful, that one's zipper doesn't close all the way."

"Thank you," I said, offering my hand.

She took it, and I saw her eyes travel down to the scrape marks on my knuckles.

"Thank you," she said.

I stuffed the envelope down into the bag and made my way out of the bank before she could call me back or alert an officer to follow me. The last thing I needed was to have a cop follow me around.

Getting in contact with the gang might have proved problematic since I didn't have anyone's number had it not been for a car parked right at the entrance of the parking lot of the hotel. I laughed mirth-lessly to myself when I saw it and who was sitting in the driver's seat. It was the bald one, sporting his own black eye and a bandage covering a place on his forehead where Lila had struck him with a projectile rock.

He was sitting there for a purpose. He was trying to intimidate me. To remind me that I had two ways out and that he was going to see to it that I followed one of them. Or else. But with the bag of money in my hand and a sudden, intense anger in my belly, I decided to turn it on him. I marched right up to the car and knocked on the window.

"Here you go," I said, holding out the envelope. We were in full view of a camera over the parking lot, and I watched his eyes float up to it before he snapped the envelope out of my hand.

"What the fuck, kid?" he growled.

"It's all there," I said. "Twenty K. I just had it counted out at the bank, so don't try to fuck with me. It's all there."

He looked from me to the envelope and back a few times like a con-fused caveman.

"So you're not going to throw the game?" he asked.

"No, dumbass," I said.

"What did you call me?" he thundered.

"I called you a dumbass," I repeated. "Now listen to me. I don't give a *fuck* what happens to my dad from now on. Or my mom. As far as they are concerned, I don't fucking exist. This is every dime I had, so I am no good to you in any way. They won't do shit for me, so you can't threaten to hurt me to get to them, and I seriously could give a shit from now on if you do threaten to hurt them. I'm done with them. This is their fucking problem now. But you are paid up. Leave them alone until they make another dumb-fuck mistake. And leave me alone. For-ever."

He sat there, blinking for a moment, and I could almost see the wheels turning in his head. He was trying to decide if he wanted to be angry at me or not. To try to force some respect out of me or something. But then I saw him notice my black eye, and it was like the memory of just how bad he and his boys had gotten their ass kicked hit him. It was just the two of us in that parking lot at the moment. In broad daylight.

He was either going to have to shoot me or leave me alone. Any other response was going to end with him getting his ass handed to him, and he knew it.

Then a smirk crossed his lips. It was sickening. He had won, and he had done the calculations, however slowly, to figure it out.

"Thank you for your business," he said. "From now on, as far as we're concerned, you don't exist. Unless you need to borrow some money someday."

"I won't," I said.

"Good," he said. "Have a good life, kid."

"I will now," I said.

As he drove away, I had to hold back the desire to kick at the taillight of his car.

Heading inside, twenty thousand dollars poorer and angry as hell, I grabbed another orange juice and a couple of slices of bacon from the breakfast bar and headed upstairs, munching on them. The game wouldn't be until this evening, but I had some energy to work out.

I WAS UPSTAIRS, STRETCHING and mentally preparing myself for the game. Or at least trying to. Every time my mind felt like it was focused on my scouting report, Lila would appear in my thoughts, and everything would go haywire. Sighing, I pulled my phone to me, thinking I should at least try to text her. She was probably already on the fields, considering her team played an hour ahead of mine. But maybe she would have a message to get back to.

As soon as I opened the phone, though, the notification from Star stuck out at me. I needed to deal with that. Sooner rather than later. And before I could do anything else with Lila.

I opened it and stared at the short message. Another mirthless laugh fell out of my lips.

So it was like that.

"I agree. Bye Gavin."

That was it. Four words. And just like that, the relationship, whatever kind of relationship it had really been, was done.

I didn't know if I was angry or relieved. Or sad. But I did know I was going to pitch.

My arm felt like fire and hatred, but I had a need to hurl a baseball as hard as I could. I was going to finish getting dressed, go down to the field, and tell Coach I'd fallen down some steps but that I was good to go. To give me the fucking ball. That I wanted to strike some people out tonight.

Kevin wouldn't contradict me. He was the kind of guy that would stand by while I made a horrifyingly stupid decision, then help pick up the pieces when I fell apart. I was going to trust him to guide my adrenaline through a game tonight, and if I couldn't go, if I was a detriment to the team, he would be the one to tell Coach to pull me.

But I was going to throw until my arm fell off otherwise.

I grabbed my bat bag, throwing it over my good shoulder, and headed down to the locker room the second I was fully dressed. The gym was empty already, and guys were heading to the field. I followed them, spotting Kevin in the distance. Most of them were going to the girls' field to watch them play for a bit first.

As I passed the field where the girls' team was going, I saw Lila on the mound. She didn't notice me. I wanted to keep moving, to head out to the field and focus. But my mind arrested me right there. I couldn't stop staring at her.

She fired in a strike, ending the inning with a strikeout-looking. She pumped her fist and roared as she headed to the benches, and I felt a little part of me cheer with her.

Then I looked down at the ground and started heading to my own field. I passed right by the bleachers where she sat, but I didn't say a word to her.

I wondered if I ever would again.

## THE END

THE WRONG SIDE OF THE TRACKS #3
THE
FIGHTBACK
USA TODAY BESTSELLING AUTHOR
LEXY TIMMS

# The Wrong Side of the Tracks

The Knockback
The Overshare
The Fightback

# Find Lexy Timms:

**Lexy Timms Newsletter:**
http://www.lexytimms.com/newsletter
**Lexy Timms Facebook Page:**
https://www.facebook.com/LexyTimmsAuthor
**Lexy Timms Website:**
http://www.lexytimms.com

Lexy Timms
BOSS
Book 3
BOSS
Book 2
BOSS
Book 1
Managing the
BOSSES
Books 1-3
Lexy Timms
FREE
for a
Limited
Time

Want

# FREE READS?

Sign up for Lexy Timms' newsletter
And she'll send you updates on new releases,
ARC copies of books and a whole lotta fun!
Sign up for news and updates!
http://www.lexytimms.com/newsletter

# More by Lexy Timms:

*FROM BEST SELLING AUTHOR, Lexy Timms, comes a billionaire romance that'll make you swoon and fall in love all over again.*

Jamie Connors has given up on men. Despite being smart, pretty, and just slightly overweight, she's a magnet for the kind of guys that don't stay around.

Her sister's wedding is at the foreground of the family's attention. Jamie would be fine with it if her sister wasn't pressuring her to lose weight so she'll fit in the maid of honor dress, her mother would get off her case and her ex-boyfriend wasn't about to become her brother-in-law.

Determined to step out on her own, she accepts a PA position from billionaire Alex Reid. The job includes an apartment on his property and gets her out of living in her parent's basement.

Jamie must balance her life and somehow figure out how to manage her billionaire boss, without falling in love with him.

** The Boss is book 1 in the Managing the Bosses series. All your questions won't be answered in the first book. It may end on a cliff hanger.

*For mature audiences only. There are adult situations, but this is a love story, NOT erotica.*

THE ONE YOU CAN'T FORGET

Emily Rose Dougherty is a good Catholic girl from mythical Walkerville, CT. She had somehow managed to get herself into a heap trouble with the law, all because an ex-boyfriend has decided to make things difficult.

Luke "Spade" Wade owns a Motorcycle repair shop and is the Road Captain for Hades' Spawn MC. He's shocked when he reads in the paper that his old high school flame has been arrested. She's always been the one he couldn't forget.

Will destiny let them find each other again? Or what happens in the past, best left for the history books?

*** This is book 1 of the Hades' Spawn MC Series. All your questions may not be answered in the first book.*

A Burning Love Series

Book 1 – Spark of Passion
Book 2 – Flame of Desire
Book 3 – Blaze of Ecstasy

A Maybe Series

Book 1 – Maybe I Should
Book 2 – Maybe I Shouldn't
Book 3 – Maybe I Did

# Don't miss out!

Visit the website below and you can sign up to receive emails whenever Lexy Timms publishes a new book. There's no charge and no obligation.

https://books2read.com/r/B-A-NNL-CZEZB

BOOKS 2 READ

Connecting independent readers to independent writers.

Did you love *The Overshare*? Then you should read *Troubled Nate Thomas - Part 1*[1] by Lexy Timms!

*Bestselling romance author, Lexy Timms, brings you a new sport romance series that'll blow your mind—it's dynamite!*

**"TNT" – Troubled Nate Thomas...**

Dubbed so by the media because Nate's always getting into trouble. Talented, handsome, and halfway out the door, Nate Thomas is on his last chance with the Denver Broncos. No one will deny he's got skills—on the field and in the bedroom. However, his taste for the party lifestyle, his drinking, and his anger issues are putting his career in jeopardy.

Coach Johnson wants his starting quarterback to actually play the way his big-money contract states he can. He needs to find a way to get

---

1. https://books2read.com/u/bP1LyR

2. https://books2read.com/u/bP1LyR

Nate's head back in the game. Threats, fines, and tickets don't seem to even slow Nate down.

With no choice but to try and risk the impossible, Coach Johnson hires a babysitter to look after Nate.

Amanda Jones is desperate for a job to help pay for her final year of her Master's. She's got a thesis to write and thinks being an au pair is the easiest way to get her work done, while making good money. She's stunned when she finds out she'll be taking care the infamous trouble-maker, Nate Thomas, aka TNT.

The money's too good to say no to, but can she somehow convince this train-wreck of an athlete to get his crap together before they both destroy the one thing they're good at?

Read more at www.lexytimms.com.

# Also by Lexy Timms

**12 Days of Christmas**
Snowflake Hollow - Part 1
Snowflake Hollow - Part 2
Snowflake Hollow - Part 3
Snowflake Hollow - Part 4
Snowflake Hollow - Part 5
Snowflake Hollow - Part 6
Snowflake Hollow - Part 7
Snowflake Hollow - Part 8
Snowflake Hollow - Part 9
Snowflake Hollow - Part 10
Snowflake Hollow - Part 11
Snowflake Hollow - Part 12
Snowflake Hollow - Complete Series

**A Bad Boy Bullied Romance**
I Hate You
I Hate You A Little Bit
I Hate You A Little Bit More

**A Bump in the Road Series**
Expecting Love
Selfless Act
Doctor's Orders

**A Burning Love Series**
Spark of Passion
Flame of Desire
Blaze of Ecstasy

**A Chance at Forever Series**
Forever Perfect
Forever Desired
Forever Together

**A Dark Casino Romance Series**
High Roller
Place Your Bet
All Or Nothing

**A Dark Mafia Romance Series**
Taken By The Mob Boss
Truce With The Mob Boss
Taking Over the Mob Boss

Trouble For The Mob Boss
Tailored By The Mob Boss
Tricking the Mob Boss


**A Dating App Series**
I've Been Matched
You've Been Matched
We've Been Matched


**A "Kind of" Billionaire**
Taking a Risk
Safety in Numbers
Pretend You're Mine


**A Maybe Series**
Maybe I Should
Maybe I Shouldn't
Maybe I Did


**A Royal Affair Series**
Royally F*cked
Royally Screwed
Royally Obsessed


**Assisting the Boss Series**

Billion Reasons
Duke of Delegation
Late Night Meetings
Delegating Love
Suitors and Admirers


**BBW Romance Series**
Capturing Her Beauty
Pursuing Her Dreams
Tracing Her Curves


**Beating the Biker Series**
Making Her His
Making the Break
Making of Them


**Betrayal at the Bay Series**
Devil's Bay
Devil's Deceit
Devil's Duplicity


**Billionaire Banker Series**
Banking on Him
Price of Passion
Investing in Love
Knowing Your Worth

Treasured Forever
Banking on Christmas
Billionaire Banker Box Set Books #1-3

**Billionaire CEO Brothers**
Tempting the Player
Late Night Boardroom
Reviewing the Perfomance
Result of Passion
Directing the Next Move
Touching the Assets

**Billionaire Hitman Series**
The Hit
The Job
The Run

**Billionaire Holiday Romance Series**
Driving Home for Christmas
The Valentine Getaway
Cruising Love
Billionaire Holiday Romance Box Set

**Billionaire in Disguise Series**
Facade
Illusion

Charade

**Billionaire Secrets Series**
The Secret
Freedom
Courage
Trust
Impulse
Billionaire Secrets Box Set Books #1-3

**Blind Sight Series**
See Me
Fix Me
Eyes On Me

**Branded Series**
Money or Nothing
What People Say
Give and Take

**Building Billions**
Building Billions - Part 1
Building Billions - Part 2
Building Billions - Part 3

**Butler & Heiress Series**
To Serve
For Duty
No Chore
All Wrapped Up


**Change of Heart Series**
The Heart Needs
The Heart Wants
The Heart Knows


**Club Confession Series**
Envy
Crave
Decoy
Urge
Oath
Club Confession Box Set Books #1-3


**Cottage by the Sea Series**
Surging Tide
Distant Shores
Twisting Ocean

**Counting the Billions**
Counting the Days
Counting On You
Counting the Kisses


**Cry Wolf Reverse Harem Series**
Beautiful & Wild
Misunderstood
Never Tamed


**Darkest Night Series**
Savage
Vicious
Brutal
Sinful
Fierce


**Diamond in the Rough Anthology**
Billionaire Rock
Billionaire Rock - part 2


**Dirty Little Taboo Series**
Flirting Touch
Denying Pleasure

Forbidding Desire
Craving Passion


**Dominating PA Series**
Her Personal Assistant - Part 1
Her Personal Assistant - Part 2
Her Personal Assistant Box Set


**Fake Billionaire Series**
Faking It
Temporary CEO
Caught in the Act
Never Tell A Lie
Fake Christmas
Fake Billionaire Box Set #1-3


**Firehouse Romance Series**
Caught in Flames
Burning With Desire
Craving the Heat
Firehouse Romance Complete Collection


**Forging Billions Series**
Dirty Money
Petty Cash
Payment Required

**For His Pleasure**
Elizabeth

Georgia

Madison


**Fortune Riders MC Series**
Billionaire Biker

Billionaire Ransom

Billionaire Misery

Fortune Riders Box Set - Books #1-3


**Fragile Series**
Fragile Touch

Fragile Kiss

Fragile Love


**Great Temptation Series**
The Devil's Footsteps

Heaven's Command

Mortals Surrender


**Hades' Spawn Motorcycle Club**
One You Can't Forget

One That Got Away

One That Came Back
One You Never Leave
One Christmas Night
Hades' Spawn MC Complete Series

**Hard Rocked Series**
Rhyme
Harmony
Lyrics

**Heart of Stone Series**
The Protector
The Guardian
The Warrior

**Heart of the Battle Series**
Celtic Viking
Celtic Rune
Celtic Mann
Heart of the Battle Series Box Set

**Heistdom Series**
Master Thief
Goldmine
Diamond Heist
Smile For Me

Your Move
Green With Envy
Saving Money


**Highlander Wolf Series**
Pack Run
Pack Land
Pack Rules


**Hollyweird Fae Series**
Inception of Gold
Disruption of Magic
Guardians of Twilight


**How To Love A Spy**
The Secret
The Secret Life
The Secret Wife


**Just About Series**
About Love
About Truth
About Forever
Just About Box Set Books #1-3

**Justice Series**
Seeking Justice
Finding Justice
Chasing Justice
Pursuing Justice
Justice - Complete Series


**Karma Series**
Walk Away
Make Him Pay
Perfect Revenge


**King of Hades MC Series**
Sinner
Tempting Sinner
Enticing Sinner


**Kissed by Billions**
Kissed by Passion
Kissed by Desire
Kissed by Love


**Leaning Towards Trouble**
Trouble

Discord
Tenacity


**Love on the Sea Series**
Ships Ahoy
Rough Sea
High Tide


**Lovers in London Series**
Risking Millions
Venture Capital
Worth the Expense
The Price of Luxury
Exclusive Passion
Sparkling Christmas
Lovers in London - 3 Book Box Set


**Love You Series**
Love Life
Need Love
My Love


**Managing the Billionaire**
Never Enough
Worth the Cost
Secret Admirers

Chasing Affection
Pressing Romance
Timeless Memories
Managing the Billionaire Box Set Books #1-3


**Managing the Bosses Series**
The Boss
The Boss Too
Who's the Boss Now
Love the Boss
I Do the Boss
Wife to the Boss
Employed by the Boss
Brother to the Boss
Senior Advisor to the Boss
Forever the Boss
Christmas With the Boss
Billionaire in Control
Billionaire Makes Millions
Billionaire at Work
Precious Little Thing
Priceless Love
Valentine Love
The Cost of Freedom
Trick or Treat
The Night Before Christmas
Gift for the Boss - Novella 3.5
Managing the Bosses Box Set #1-3
Managing the Bosses Novellas

**Mislead by the Bad Boy Series**
Deceived
Provoked
Betrayed

**Model Mayhem Series**
Shameless
Modesty
Imperfection

**Moment in Time**
Highlander's Bride
Victorian Bride
Modern Day Bride
A Royal Bride
Forever the Bride

**Mountain Millionaire Series**
Close to the Ridge
Crossing the Bluff
Climbing the Mount

**My Best Friend's Sister**
Hometown Calling

A Perfect Moment
Thrown in Together


**My Darker Side Series**
Darkest Hour
Time to Stop
Against the Light


**Neverending Dream Series**
Neverending Dream - Part 1
Neverending Dream - Part 2
Neverending Dream - Part 3
Neverending Dream - Part 4
Neverending Dream - Part 5
Neverending Dream Box Set Books #1-3


**Outside the Octagon**
Submit
Fight
Knockout


**Protecting Diana Series**
Her Bodyguard
Her Defender
Her Champion
Her Protector

Her Forever
Protecting Diana Box Set Books #1-3

**Protecting Layla Series**
His Mission
His Objective
His Devotion

**Racing Hearts Series**
Rush
Pace
Fast

**Regency Romance Series**
The Duchess Scandal - Part 1
The Duchess Scandal - Part 2

**Reverse Harem Series**
Primals
Archaic
Unitary

**Roommate Wanted Series**
The Roommate
The Bunkmate

The Flatmate

**R&S Rich and Single Series**
Alex Reid
Parker
Sebastian
Zane


**Saving Forever**
Saving Forever - Part 1
Saving Forever - Part 2
Saving Forever - Part 3
Saving Forever - Part 4
Saving Forever - Part 5
Saving Forever - Part 6
Saving Forever Part 7
Saving Forever - Part 8
Saving Forever Boxset Books #1-3


**Secrets & Lies Series**
Strange Secrets
Evading Secrets
Inspiring Secrets
Lies and Secrets
Mastering Secrets
Alluring Secrets
Secrets & Lies Box Set Books #1-3

**Shifting Desires Series**
Jungle Heat
Jungle Fever
Jungle Blaze


**Sin Series**
Payment for Sin
Atonement Within
Declaration of Love


**Southern Romance Series**
Little Love Affair
Siege of the Heart
Freedom Forever
Soldier's Fortune


**Spanked Series**
Passion
Playmate
Pleasure


**Spelling Love Series**
The Author
The Book Boyfriend

The Words of Love

**Strength & Style**
Suits You, Sir
Tailor Made
Perfect Gentleman

**Taboo Wedding Series**
He Loves Me Not
With This Ring
Happily Ever After

**Tattooist Series**
Confession of a Tattooist
Surrender of a Tattooist
Heart of a Tattooist
Hopes & Dreams of a Tattooist

**Tennessee Romance**
Whisky Lullaby
Whisky Melody
Whisky Harmony

**The Bad Boy Alpha Club**
Battle Lines - Part 1

Battle Lines

**The Brush Of Love Series**
Every Night
Every Day
Every Time
Every Way
Every Touch
The Brush of Love Series Box Set Books #1-3


**The City of Mayhem Series**
True Mayhem
Relentless Chaos
Broken Disorder


**The Debt**
The Debt: Part 1 - Damn Horse
The Debt: Complete Collection


**The Fire Inside Series**
Dare Me
Defy Me
Burn Me


**The Gentleman's Club Series**

Gambler
Player
Wager


**The Golden Game**
On The Pitch
Respect the Game
All Game
Sweat and Tears
The Final Score
The Golden Game Box Set Books #1-3


**The Golden Mail**
Hot Off the Press
Extra! Extra!
Read All About It
Stop the Press
Breaking News
This Just In
The Golden Mail Box Set Books #1-3


**The Lucky Billionaire Series**
Lucky Break
Streak of Luck
Lucky in Love

**The Millionaire's Pretty Woman Series**
Perfect Stranger
Captive Devotion
Sweet Temptations


**The Sound of Breaking Hearts Series**
Disruption
Destroy
Devoted


**The University of Gatica Series**
The Recruiting Trip
Faster
Higher
Stronger
Dominate
No Rush
University of Gatica - The Complete Series


**The Wrong Side of the Tracks**
The Knockback
The Overshare


**Timing is Everything Series**

Right Time
Right Place
Right Reasons


**T.N.T. Series**
Troubled Nate Thomas - Part 1
Troubled Nate Thomas - Part 2
Troubled Nate Thomas - Part 3


**Toxic Touch Series**
Noxious
Lethal
Willful
Tainted
Craved
Toxic Touch Box Set Books #1-3


**Undercover Boss Series**
Marketing
Finance
Legal


**Undercover Series**
Perfect For Me
Perfect For You
Perfect For Us

**Unknown Identity Series**
Unknown
Unpublished
Unexposed
Unsure
Unwritten
Unknown Identity Box Set: Books #1-3


**Unlucky Series**
Unlucky in Love
UnWanted
UnLoved Forever


**War Torn Letters Series**
My Sweetheart
My Darling
My Beloved


**Wet & Wild Series**
Stormy Love
Savage Love
Secure Love


**Worth It Series**

Worth Billions
Worth Every Cent
Worth More Than Money


**You & Me - A Bad Boy Romance**
Just Me
Touch Me
Kiss Me


**Standalone**
Wash
Loving Charity
Summer Lovin'
Love & College
Billionaire Heart
First Love
Frisky and Fun Romance Box Collection
Beating Hades' Bikers
Everyone Loves a Bad Boy
Dead of Night


Watch for more at www.lexytimms.com.

# About the Author

"Love should be something that lasts forever, not is lost forever." Visit USA TODAY BESTSELLING AUTHOR, LEXY TIMMS https://www.facebook.com/SavingForever *Please feel free to connect with me and share your comments. I love connecting with my readers.* Sign up for news and updates and freebies - I like spoiling my readers! http://eepurl.com/9i0vD website: www.lexytimms.com Dealing in Antique Jewelry and hanging out with her awesome hubby and three kids, Lexy Timms loves writing in her free time. MANAGING THE BOSSES is a bestselling 10-part series dipping into the lives of Alex Reid and Jamie Connors. Can a secretary really fall for her billionaire boss?

Read more at www.lexytimms.com.